NOT B[
and O

Cliff G Hanley

ISBN 13: 1978-484986745
ISBN 10: 1484986741

Also by Cliff G Hanley:
The Red Guitar
Springheeled Kate
Palestine Incidentally
Palestine for Beginners
www.cliff-g-hanley.com

contents

CLIFF G HANLEY

Not Being Dead

For Lee, whose intervention took me from my easel and got me writing again: and for all those with whom I collided and those I missed - you know who you are.

CLIFF G HANLEY

Not Being Dead

CLIFF G HANLEY

One

he picked up the card. It had fallen out of the envelope as he tore at it, recognising as his thumbnail sliced under the gum-strip, the heavy presence inside of another 'special offer' from the soggy pizza company. Not...

"Dear *Henry*   You are cordially invited to celebrate the wedding of Eleanor and Gwilym."

Gwilym! He's a fucking architect! And she's married him! What's she doing, getting married, anyway? No-one gets married anymore. And didn't her mother finish it off for us all, marrying all those artists and writing that evil poetry about them afterwards? Hmm?

Henry slouched on back from the hall to the kitchen, picking up his dressing gown from the floor as he went. It felt damp from the bare floorboards, but it was better than naked.

The milk wasn't off, yet. It wouldn't matter anyway, with muesli, but black coffee first thing in the morning was definitely out. While consuming a leisurely breakfast, he read the invitation again, slowly. Appraised the design of the card. Not bad. Almost frame-worthy; built by hand. Looked up. The back view, so familiar it was wallpaper - red brick, moss, treetop waving at the clouds. The day ahead. Overhead. Looming. The loom of life. One month since the ceramics department closed, followed by early retirement. He could have taken over graphics, though. They were blatantly unenthusiastic about that option. He knew he had lacked diplomacy when it came to talking about the college's increasing tendency towards so-called new media and similar shite.

"Look for the big flag in Blomfield Road. Fais Deaux Belle will depart from Little Venice on Saturday 12th at 2pm, to arrive at the Leghorn at 4pm with celebrations in poetry and song."

'What, do they expect us to sing?'
'No, Stella, I think they will have something organised for the boat.'
'Oh, that'll be a shame. D'you think Henry will be there too?'

Expelling cigarette smoke, Oscar Early threw himself back into his armchair and stared at the blank TV screen,'No doubt. If they asked him, he will go. I know my brother. He's not cut out to be a loner. I'll call him in a while.'

Henry back from the shops. Welcomed by the plaintive toots of his answering machine.
'You have one new message. Message one: Monday ten a.m. "It's Oscar here. You towny - out again, and it's only ten in the morning. One time I'll call you and perhaps you will pick up the phone." End of messages.'

Oaf calls me a 'towny' just because they live out in Chiswick. They call it London.

Going back out, left past the new, slow down to breathe in, tandoori place; left again to Portobello Road and the pub.
'Well well, good morning. You're up early today!'
'Not as early as you think. It's just the bags round my eyes.'
'Ha ha! So,' - clapping and rubbing hands- 'what'll it be, then?'
'Um, a pint of IPA should do for a start, please.'
'Coming up!'

The newspaper. More stuff about the telly and their jobs. Nothing about Oscar, though. How many in-house producers have they got left, now? Bloody America. We should call the government the Labor Party. Remember that one. She's nice. It's the eyes. Looks intelligent. And firm...

The door swung open: customer two. Jerry Parkin weaved in and edged towards the bar.
'A Kronenbourg. Pint. Ta' -slamming cash on the counter; scooped up and into the drawer
schhtoom cadunk - a non-expressive return slam of change
Elbow on bar, he twisted round to Henry.
'Heyyy, long time no see.'
'No, I've been... making some changes in my life.'
'Cool. Need any stuff?'
'Probably not, thanks. I think I'll take it easy all round.'
'Fair enough. You still teaching?'
'No, I've chucked that.'
'But the studio?'
'Still using the studio though.'
'Shepherd's Bush?'
'Yes'
'Who's that girl, Maria, she says it might be coming down.'
'Well, there was a rumour it might be demolished, but it's okay - the potters live on.'
'The potters, eh? Ha!'

Henry's openness towards Jerry was mostly from habit; he deeply regretted having revealed the studio's address to him. At the time it seemed like a convenience, having the kid drop in with a regular supply of good dope at a fair price, and it increased his standing with his fellow (and younger) artists, but the boy was a bit too matey sometimes (or was it just that Henry was getting old?) and the whiff of the underworld he carried had long since lost its glamour, as the possibility of a brush with The Law grew more likely for 'people like us.'

'So! What d'you think? Gwil! Look at the back!' Eleanor twirled round, arms raised.
'Jeeziz,' said Gwilym, 'should you wear that in public?'
'Haha! I shouldn't even let you see it yet. Bad luck, isn't it?'
'Oh Baby, I don't care!'

Blissfully unaware of the torrid deep-pile carpet scene playing out merely fortyfive minutes' walk from the kiln he shares with two other craftsmen, failed suitor Henry keeps a steady hand as he throws another slightly avant-garde pot.

'Henery! What on earth brought you out here?'
Oscar looking down from his front door, ushering Henry inside.

'I got your message. Whining again. I finished early at the studio tonight anyway. I'm thinking of getting rid of this old car - tonight could be my last trip for a while.'

'Well, what kind of life are you living now? Without Angela, the job, and no car too?'

'What'll I need a car for, now? There's no bloody place to park it, and I can get the Tube everywhere.'

'I bet you would've just gone home, if you weren't mobile.'

'We-ell. Yes. I just turned off to Hammersmith as a bit of a whim.'

'What do you mean, whining?'

'That stuff about me being out again.' -Henry walked into the living room, sprawled heavily on the couch- 'You sound so different from your telly self, it's fucking funny.'

'You're talking about being professional. That's what it's all about. And you sound like a fucking whiner too, when you get going. Stella!'

'I'm still fixing the curtain!'

'She's up there, doing the D.I.Y. Want a drink?' -walking through the little hallway, across the living room to the shelf behind the sofa. The television silently flooding its end of the room in irritated blue.

'Sure. Is this whisky?'

'Of course. You didn't think it was sherry did you? ...Glasgow left its mark in a few ways.'

'That was only a year.'

'More than a year, remember. Long enough to learn the trade. And enough to learn serious drinking, hah! Well.'

Henry drank.

'Did you see my show on Sunday?'

'Yes. I did. -Where did you get all that stuff about funk art? I thought it had died out in 1970.'

'Well, you see it didn't - the name just changed, and it stopped being cutting-edge, as far as the critics were concerned. I expected you to catch it, as so much of it was about ceramics. The guy practically walked in out of the blue.'

'Well, who the hell cares what the critics...'

'It's all grist to the mill...'

'Yes, I saw the listing. I couldn't do your job, you know. You give terms like 'cutting-edge' some kind of credibility.'

'Well, you know, you can change the meaning by changing its context...'

'Context! That's another one!'

'..in time or place.' -'And who says a blue painting's more or less blue if it's in a gallery or on a shelf?' -'And one trope aught to be just as viable, as significant, as any other. That means the traditional beside the language of ideas.'

'Ideas? Are they separate from paint? You can't imagine how many ideas go into just one picture or sculpture.'

'Yah yah, I'll bet I can, but - you know - art can grow from the idea to the concept, as an end in itself.'

'Some end. Anyway, 'simportant to keep the meaning as it is, it's a language we use, so we can understand each other. And when some bugger shifts the goalposts...'

'Well, now, you can't do a Pol Pot - that's a good one - and stick to cave painting.'

'...' Henry thinking about white rooms and skips

'And traditional forms of expression don't have to be more meaningful than new media-'

'For traditional, read art. Fuck's sake, you used to sound more like a hippy; where did you-'

'So did you. But don't get hung up on phenomenology - you want to...'

'Phenomenology? You mean stuff, or things?'

'No - not really - it's about interior consciousness.'

'Well, it doesn't sound like it. Shouldn't consciousness be about reacting to phenomenons? Phenomena? Things?'

'Well, now' -Oscar standing, reaching for the whisky bottle on the cane-fronted bar and refilling both their glasses as he sat again- 'there *is* a theory of language and culture. A relational theory. And *meaning* can come out of the buzz between cultures, media.'

He stood back, frowning at the bar. Henry carried on, 'If you like to fart about with theories, it's okay with me. But I object to people passing themselves off as artists when they just stick a bit of junk in an empty room and hand out bits of paper explaining what it fucking means.'

'What d'you mean by *means*?'

'Ask me about fucking; or *stuff*...'

Oscar leaned down behind the bar. There was a click, the glass top lit up in a pale green and pink swirl, giving some of its life to the bottles on top.

'Stuff?'- Oscar looked up again, 'Oh, Stella.'

Stella framed in the door, navy boiler suit, one size too big and big blackhair flecked with white paint, or maybe plaster, hips thrust to one side, holding a spanner like a cocktail glass

'Henry, what a surprise. Have you been working? Are you going to that party?'

'Ah, the wedding thing you mean...'

'Yes. Might be good. Want coffee?'

Oscar adding 'Look, you'd be best staying the night. In fact, you can give me a lift tomorrow. If the car starts. Top up?'

'Thanks. And yes, coffee would be good, too, thanks, Stella.'

'Won't be long!'

'Well, now, Herry, it's a rare thing for you to drag yourself out here.'

'I don't have to bother about the college anymore, of course. I'm slowly getting used to the luxury of it.

...Okay. Nothing, really... I haven't been out to the sticks for a bit.'

'Well, that's true. So you heard about the, uh, upcoming wedding? I tried phoning you to ask about it.'

'Yeah - that's - I have.'

Stella left them for the kitchen

'So you got the message. You could have called back…'

'Yeah, I could have. Never got round to it, though.'

'Maybe if you'd done more time on the stall instead of homework, you could be better organised.'

'Oh for fuck's sake! Are you going to do that again?'

'Do what?' - Oscar assuming a puzzled/ amused look

'The bloody schoolteacher line was almost funny-'

'Wasn't meant to be funny-'

'Almost. Wadda ya mean?' - Henry leaning forward

'I mean, I…' - 'It was okay sometimes, but we didn't always have stuff that sold,' Henry interrupted. Oscar was becoming annoyed- 'When I said it, it fucking mattered.'

'Remember the clock faces,' smiled Henry

'That was your idea.'

'Never was! You fucking bought them-'

'Huh! Of course, you really know about making stuff that sells, now.'

'Oh, look. Art you know about. Vocation. At least teaching was a real job.'

'And meeja ain't?

Stella, having filled the cafetiere, sat down at the kitchen table for a moment. Listened to 'the boys' as their voices rose and fell, their old arguments about family segueing into their newly-old arguments about what constituted art. She rolled a small grass joint, lit it with a match from the box on the table and smoked it. Feet on table. Head back. Breathe out slow-ly. It's been ages since I saw Henry. Wish he'd stayed away. Oscar. I know what he's been getting up to with those studio girls. Him and his big cufflinks. The funny thing is: I don't really care, any more. We're old hippies, after all. I am, anyway. There they go, shouting again! I'll roll just one more ... mm... coffee's getting cold. Drink a little, anyway. Black coffee and cigarettes. I should get into singing again. Fuck him and his dignity. If I can finish this one I'd better get to bed. It's nicer with the hand-rolled. Mellow. Get some tomorrow...

'Stella!' Oscar's sudden head through the door, 'you okay? in here? How's the coffee?'

Stella waved the cafetiere at him.

'It's cold.'

'Cold? Christ, have we been at it that long?'

She sighed, 'Never mind honey. I'm off to bed, anyway.'

'Okay, you do that. I'll uh, fix the sofa for Henry.'

'Christ! Did you have to choose Harrow Road at this time?' groaned Oscar.

'Well, I like it,' said Henry, pulling at the wheel. ' I like the old bits that are still standing, and we can turn off at Ladbroke Grove anyway. Too bad about the cemetery - it was lovely when it was full of nettles and weeds - now it's all cleared up, you have to join a guided tour.'

'Really?' Oscar's professional ears pricking up.

'Well, so I've heard.'

'Ah, the Grove... Now I can understand why you want rid of this rust heap. I told you to get a Real Car ages ago.'

'Hey, *fuck off*. I'm not one of your little researchers.' he yanked the wheel to avoid a cyclist- 'What's the point? It'd just get ripped open, smashed or stolen.'

'Well that's the price you have to pay for living in the inner city.'

'This is about as close as we can get for parking.'

The 2CV grindwobbling to a halt by the Tabernacle. Oscar decanting his shoulder bag, they walked back to Henry's.

'You were well advised to buy this when you did.'

'Well *advised*? You sound like a fucking correspondent.'

'I *am* a fucking correspondent.'

'I mean-'

'I know what you mean. Touchy boy.'

' Talking about yourself again. Well. Yes, it was Angela put me up to it.'

'She-'

'Yes, and her bloody money, too.'

'And her money-'

'Look, you know she only *had* that bloody money. I had to work for mine.'

'Teaching? Not so bad-'

'I never wanted to be a teacher.'

'Not what you said in the old days-'

'I did what I had to.'

'At least you had job security- 'Security! Just a little bit boring. And for too fucking long.'

'Okayyy. -Well now, I've a good few hours to while away before my plane. I'll look in.'

'D'you want to? Well... okay - you might as well.'

Oscar slowly turned round from the front door and looked up at the walls.

'God! I haven't been here... since...'

'Since the funeral you mean.'

'Yes. It's changed some.' nose wrinkled, sniffing

'I do some of my work here-'

'But it's - Christ! Herry - you could do with clearing up some of this mess!'

'Really? I'd just... got used to it.'

'Look - Stella found a small company - it's just a couple of people - they could clean up for you - they charge us thirty quid a week.'

'All very well - but this is a machine for working as well as a machine for living.'

'Hah! It's less Le Corbusier, more like Steptoe! Couldn't you separate the important heaps from the green mould...'

'Green mould? Where?'

'Henry. There isn't any green mould. Jesus - what's all this stuff in the sink? Look - I missed your birthday. I'll book Catpyjamas for a proper clean. They call it a 'blitz'. Have it on me.'

…

'I kind of like it like this, You Know.'

'Look, it's your birthday present.'

'Well… thanks a million but I've three months to go yet…' lowering his head into his open palm, rubbing gently -'So when do you get back from Belgium?'

'Not sure, but I'll be at the party. At Little Venice. Look - I'm going to head off to the Tube - no point in being late.'

'I'll let you get on then. I'd come down there too, but my head's starting to get a little bit painful.'

'Hah! Evil isn't it? Whisky really gets to the hub.'

'I didn't have that much…'

'Herry. What are we to do with you? You're the bohemian of the family for chrissake.'

Henry could see that his brother was taking advantage of his hangover to out-alpha him, and it was too early in the day for full-blooded exchanges. As soon as Oscar had gone, he relaxed and shut the front door, walking along the narrow hall past the stairs leading up to the bedroom and back through the cluttered kitchen to the one-time dining-room, which by increments had become a studio; although there were so many old newspapers, magazines, bits of packaging and little pieces of junk rescued from skips or even bought from junk shops, wall-to-wall, that there was no realistic demarcation between rooms and their functions. Away from the bright, functional strip light of the kitchen, he dived at the old couch. It had witnessed thirty years of parties and diving and fucking; a couple of springs stuck up in the middle where it sagged - but he had grown with it. He always missed the lumps. He drew his knees up, lay on his side, head bowed, arms folded and hoped for sleep before the throbbing in his head got over the pain threshold.

He was surrounded in the gloom by little ceramic ladies, on the floor and on the table, skinny and imperious, all with the same sardonic twist in their faces, all together and each quite alone.

CLIFF G HANLEY

Two

Although the bar hadn't opened until the Fais Deaux Belle passed Royal Oak, most of the guests had drink taken before embarking. As the talk level rose from chatter towards shouting, the assembly collectively forgot that the boat was not a self-contained room, but in fact floating on a public canal. Oscar put his arm round Henry's shoulder in such a manner as to force him to join in leaning over the side of the boat away from the babble. A grimly fixed smile.

'Listen. Do me a favour. Don't call me "Ozzie" here.'

'"Ozzie"? I haven't called you that since we were kids, for fuck's sake. Anyway, what's so important about it now?'

'Nothing, really.'

'?'

'Well - okay. It's just - there are one or two people here I'd rather took me seriously.'

'You're not joking? I mean, after all, you're not famous for being *not serious*.'

'No.'

Oscar putting on his Grimly Intense Look. Henry realised that his big little brother, for all his bravado and his celebrity, was in mortal fear of losing his job.

The wedded couple, Eleanor and Gwilym, were enthroned at the stern of the boat, surrounded by their closest friends and The Golden Bystanders, now launching into a set of punky Irish calypso. Simultaneously, the grey low-hanging sky shattered and descended as heavy rain. The smokers and fresh-air freaks, who had enjoyed a brief confluence of interests at the prow, fought their way back to the canopied stern.

Oh, Corason!
I love her on the telephone
Doesn't matter if she isn't home
Just wanna hear her ansafone

When I saw her at the dance uptown
In the garden the only flame
Her hair is red and her eyes are brown
Well, I knew I had to win the game

Then she asked me if I'd like to dance
Now I knew she could read my mind
When she spoke to me I fell in love
And I felt my troubles unwind

O, Corason!
I love her on the telephone
Doesn't matter if she isn't home
Just wanna hear her ansafone

I don't care what she says to me
Just as long as she takes her time
Her voice is sweeter than little bells
Ringing jasmine in the summertime

The Belle, music still pounding, docked at Westbourne Park, and the mate, a kid of fifteen, jumped with a rope from the gunnel to the concrete landing dock . The more intrepid, or drunk, drinkers in the pub came out past the tables and benches to the canal's edge, swaying inaccurately to the rhythm. Their boneless figures parted to allow four more guests through, led by the sober and upright Arnold Pitman. As soon as they had clambered on board, hindered as much as helped by the well-meant on-board grasping and thrusting hands, the engine revved up again and they cast off. Oscar shuffled and elbowed his way round the deck towards Pitman. Although they were hardly the same generation, he liked to think they had a common interest in most things; on the strength of his TV interview ('definitive' - The Telegraph) and a drink afterwards.

Pitman caught Oscar's eye and gave him a heavy-browed acknowledgement just as the raincoated MC ushered him off to the mid-ship microphone. His male companion, a boyish, heavily built man of fifty-plus with devilish eyebrows, remained with their ladies - one elegantly grey; one blonde. He took his arms from their shoulders for a moment while he pulled his tweed hat forward to stop it dripping on his cigarette.

'Laidees and Gentlemen! By special request, our greatest living playwright' (oos and aas) 'has agreed to give this reading exclusively for your pleasure.'

Pitman stood up to the mike, without a script.

'Hello. It's a great, no, *considerable* pleasure, to be here, and a great honour to be asked to give this reading at Eleanor's and, uh, Gwilym's wedding celebration.

After all the world had put on
Maximum visibility jackets
And become indivisibly invisible
The last darkly visible man sang out
In words not entirely risible
The girl stood on the moonlit deck
Her lips were all a-quiver
She gave a cough
Her leg flew off
And floated down the river'

A short, palpable silence. An explosion of laughter and clapping. Oscar was confused, He hadn't been ready for this. Even Pitman allowed himself a little smile. His friend turned, beaming, towards Oscar.

'Surprised you, didn't he?'

'Well, yes - he did, actually.'

'You know he was...' looked aside at the elegant grey-haired lady, who cogitated for a moment, then waved her hand dismissively, uncaringly smiling.

'He had an affair with her mother, yes. How do you know each other?'

A momentary look of sophisticated weariness.

'We go back to Royal Court days - and I edited The Room...'

Christ! Bill Watkins!'

'So! Now you've got your bearings! Hehehehe!'

'I'll get you a drink. We can join the queue here.'

'I should introduce - this is Carlotta.'

'Hello. I know you from the arts prog. And Amanda, too.'

Amanda stepped forward, 'Yes. I've seen that show too, although Arnold managed to talk me out of watching much telly a long time ago.'

'Well now, it's in a constant state of flux - and the radio looks like being on the ascendant again. In the meantime... here we are. Looks like vodka all round. That all right?'

Taking the general nodding of rain-dripped heads as assent, Oscar edged past a woman in her fifties, her frizzy hairstyle huge in the manner of the Bride of Frankenstein and streaked in red. The rain had made it resemble candy floss; it hit Oscar full in the face as he grabbed the bar's edge. The skinny barman, wiping his skinny moustache, was about to give Oscar his undivided attention when there was a loud bang against the outside; he winced and ducked. Shouts of 'Hey! Heyy! What!' - he straightened up again, and he could see through the tiny porthole two boys on the other side of the railing running by the canal, vanishing into the rain on bicycles as one of them turned and shouted, 'Fack off!' The vessel looked more like a house-boat - the kind of hybrid of hulls and shacks that typified the floating des-reses of Little Venice than a credibly mobile craft, but on top of her black belly the gaggle of multicoloured bohemians, spread like the soggily congealing sauce on a burnt steak, looked like an invasion of the stupid. The boys had taken exception to the aging nonconformists enjoying themselves in such an ostentatious colour bubble and thrown a rock. Another stone had landed on the awning, but the reading, and drinking, continued regardless. A little girl, dressed under her coat in a miniature belly-dance costume of gold, stood on a wine crate to reach the mic. As they puttered past the overbearing Trellick Tower her mother provided umbrella shelter while her tiny voice peeped out her own ten-stanza eulogy. She was allowed what felt to some of the swaying revellers a small eternity, but of course no more than little girls deserve. As soon as she was finished, the babbling resumed, even louder and more frenzied than before. Several other performers lined up to read out funny or romantic doggerel but as they were all consenting adults there was no question of anyone's conversation being further interrupted.

Although it was an early autumn day, the Leghorn loomed up through the rain as a grey shadow, with only the lights in its windows promising comfort and joy. The Belle was steered in towards the jetty, and moored. As the first guests clambered on to firm ground, they found that the slimy steps leading up to the back door looked too much like a serious climb; nearly everyone headed round the muddy incline to the side of the pub. Hostess gowns became mud-soaked as high heels dug in to the little hill. Oscar grabbed the Victorian blackrusty handrail at the bottom of the steps and, stumbling, banged his face against the tightly skirted wet arse of a crop-haired brunette, who was unsure about whether to continue upwards, or merely hold on to the rail. She looked round, eyes half open, her face an impish mask of glamorous vapidity.
'Ozzay!'

Several others looked round, as Oscar smiled quickly and scuttled towards the muddy embankment. Henry helped Stella to disembark. 'Henry, strange how you're such a gentleman.'

'Well, you know I was a young fogey once.' - 'Yes, that was long before I met you' -'Well, let's climb the hill.'

'Here, give me a pull. Thanks. The first one's on me.'

The hall attached to the back of the pub was warm and dry. The tables were heaped with buffet food and bottles of wine opened at strategic points; the bar at one end dispensed a mixture of free champagne plus wine and spirits for sale, and the Big Item Steel Band filled out the ambience at the other. After the drinking and the soaking, nearly everyone, as soon as they passed through the door, made a blind grab at the food, stuffing some in their mouths as most kept talking. The music and the amplifying effect of being indoors increased the need to shout. Perhaps as many as twenty threw themselves at the dance floor, forcing the talkers to keep to the sides, where a blizzard of food particles turned to sleet as it hit their saturated clothing. Bang! On a table: a slightly camp thirty-ish man, shiny black hair hanging down one side of his face, in a damp white tuxedo, pointing his toy gun at the ceiling- 'Maaay I have your attention please, ladies and gentlemen! I would like to propose a toast to our golden couple, Eleanor and Gwilym. Eleanor is already celebrated far and wide as the *art house toast* and *queen* of the *most*. That most elegant and decorative Pillar of Art Society, who has stolen so many hearts, has now been nicked herself by that invader from the west, young Gwilym. Not content with redesigning our city, he's decided to mess with our demography too! I've been told, incidentally, that he had nothing to do with the design of that dress,'- whistles, yoops- 'you

may be surprised to hear. But with scaffolding that was made in heaven, how could it fail? All happiness! To Eleanor and Gwilym!'
'leanor n wilym'
'nor n lym'

The dancing, eatshoutdrinkshout carried on as the band took flight again. Oscar feeling his way down the corridor to the gent's, collided with a girl in her thirties headed for the ladies and waited for her to come out again.
She could roll over. She's young, not wrinkled, and drunker than me. Big eyes.
'Ah, you again. Sorry, I keep bumping into you.'
'Are you Oscar Early? It's hard to see in this light.'
(yes!) 'Yes. But tonight I'm just being... myself.' (give her the eye crinkle)
'I just caught the tail end of that Ken Russell season at the Film Theatre.'
'Did you? I covered it, you know, on my programme.'
'Ye-ahs - all the telly stuff - wossit - Isadora...' - 'Duncan,' Oscar added. She waved her fragile, bared arms in a sand-dancing pose -
'Vivienne Pickles?' he asked. She mimed neck breaking, eyes bulging. 'Marvelous. Got it in one. it was a good while back. And the Debussy Film?'
'Missed that one,' she replied, 'I remember it though - Oliver Reed-'
'the girl in the white T-shirt...'
'... he was quite young'

'Getting shot with arrows - and enjoying it'
'And enjoying it. -Was she?'
'Extraordinary. You know, the reason I
remember that one so well is, not long before
seeing it I'd had a dream that looked quite like
it...'
Raised eyebrows
'but it was a stage full of girls in white, all
posing, nubile and rigid, with bows, and
several of them shot. Hah -can't begin to
imagine where that came from!'
'Excuse me. I'm going for some fags.'

A brief vignette through the doorway to the
party room: Henry, having forced himself to
talk to Gwilym; the two blurring past '-so I
reckoned they should change it to Labor - tha's
the American way after all.' - 'Haha, not bad!'

Henry sneaking into the public bar, sees
familiar face
'Joanne. Haven't seen you for a few years.'
'No. I haven't been away or anything. Just... I
must get a coffee.' turning to the barman 'Yes -
could I have a coffee?'
'Black or white?'
'Black. I suppose I haven't been going to the
same old pubs for a bit, though.'
'I have, some of them, though I'm not with the
college any more...'
'Really? Have you gone on the telly, too?'
'No, though that's an idea.'
'You, too, sir?'

'Oh yes please - black.'

The roar of the coffee machine
Sipping the scalding black water: pub coffee at
its most cursory

'It's been so long…'
'Yes it has been a good while. More like years
than months.'
'You said you're still sculpting.'
'We-ell - I've slowed down a bit. I haven't
produced quite as much as I used to, and some
of it has been binned. The big spaces between
works mean they come out looking like they're
by different people At least the quality has
improved, I hope. And you?'
'Oh, I haven't painted for three years.'
'God! The hardest thing is getting started
again. Maybe you could have a go at something
else…'
'Writing, I could. I remember we were talking
about going for a drink…'
'Yes - where and when? there's so much to
catch up on. I've got quite a lot of free time
now…any time of the day you like. Are you
rushing back into the party already? We could
meet…'
'I can't really meet during the day at the
moment. I'm working in translation…'
'Sort of nine to five?'
'Almost. Till early afternoon. How about
Saturday?'
'Saturday I can do.'
'Ten thirty at the V&A.'

'Ten thirty it is.'

He was late. She sat, smiling, inside the entrance, and waved away his apologies; they turned and walked to the Raphael room. Although the sanguine walls were huge she found the drawings always induced a feeling of serenity.

'I couldn't believe it the first time I walked in here as a boy, finding an entire staircase left over from an Elizabethan house, but inside a museum.'

'A boy would like playing with buildings.'

'I suppose it was the mechanics...'

'Mechanics?'

'Well, more, I think, that it was a kind of magic, putting a piece of a house from the distant past into a fairly modern room...' They were passing into the next hall. 'Well, There is something about stairways. In dolls' houses or toy buses, I remember they added an element of something... interesting - the same kind of thing maybe as sexiness...'

She felt a rare sensation; a mixture of prurience and enlightenment, with just a whiff of disapproval. 'But you wouldn't know what sexiness was when you were young, would you? Why sexiness anyway?'

'I'm sure the part of my mind that switches on to some kind of vital enjoyment, got...'

'Triggered...'

'triggered by these different things, for what may be a fundamentally similar reason.'

'Tut tut - you've been thinking about this rather a lot.'

'Well, I admit, I have!' - He decided not to elaborate on the upward spiral of the stairs imitating the atavistic urge which had also found expression in tales of princes with big swords battling up through thickets to their princesses, or the value-added attraction of skirts, stockings and suspenders; he was a little afraid that he might sound boring.

'What's the time?' Henry lifted his arm and exposed his watch. 'We've only been wandering for half an hour.'

'Shall we go round, and head for the café?'

'Yes, let's do that. No hurry for me, though.'

Plugged into their table with selfserve coffee and cake, they left the world of arts and crafts, for the present.

'Joanne, I remember when you were selling that little hideaway of yours…'

'I do miss that terribly. That was ten years ago, now…'

'Ten years? Christ!'

'and you mustn't think…'

'Oh, all right. I was just thinking about it. That was a lovely time. St Ives. And I still haven't met your husband.'

'I think that's best, don't you?' smiling

Politely emerging into Cromwell Road, crinkly smiles in the unexpected sun; a warmly felt hand grasp and they went their separate ways.

Walking across the road, he stops to look up at the autumn yellow leaves, hit side-on by the icy-bright sun

If I had died and not Angela, I wouldn't enjoy these trees.
I wouldn't mind, though. The dead feel no grief. And the trees would be just as beautiful.

But would they? Beauty is perceived. And the trees. Take us away and you just have the quiet hum of... treegrow.
No. Not hum. Soundwaves maybe. Heard by herds. Do cows think about trees? If not, then - no trees.

South Kensington tube station: the side facing the sun welcomes the weary traveller into the next-door bar, where he enjoys a double whisky, neat, sipping while staring vacantly at the passing traffic...
-beep beep tweedle-eedle beep -
Grab at the mobile phone bulking in pocket
'Yes?'
'That you Henry?'
'Yes of course.'
'Well now, where are you? You haven't forgotten the cleaner's coming round today, have you?'
'Oh, fuck it, I did. When?'
'Look, Henry, I *told* you. You should have written it down. It's two o'clock. Can you handle that?'

'Oh fuck, yes. Look, this <u>was</u> your idea. I'll be there. Maybe on time.'

'Jolly good. Keep in touch.'

'Sure, sure.'

He replaced the phone. Its weight was disfiguring his jacket - he had only got the thing to avoid being sneered at by Oscar for being behind the times. He took time finishing his drink, and left, to hurry home .

Three

The thought of a complete stranger exploring his home in depth had prompted Henry to empty the rancid plates, with their patina of congealed food, out of the greasy water in the kitchen sink to a black bin-bag. One plate went straight in, being terminally conjoined to the blackened mass of old food. Having made a start, he walked round the ground floor, kicking some of the magazine heaps into another bag.

He had not been aware of the gradual slumification of his home until the imminent visit from Catspyjamas forced a return to self-consciousness. Angela used to nag him when he got sloppy.

'Henry, how long have you had these pants? Look at the state of them - holes - these ones too.'

'Henry - this table was meant to be for eating off, not for messing up.'

'Henry - you're getting a beer belly.'

For a while he had felt he could become like a bear, putting it on and getting some weight; an imposing figure of a man - but really, he was too short.

He hesitated. Black bag magneted to the floor, full of stuff he didn't really need, after all. Pages ripped out and kept sacred for their imagined links to prospective creativity, broken toys, little boxes, crockery, rescued and brought home as booty for their fleeting resemblance to half-dreamed images.

Images. He was losing himself, staring down at the crumpled pictures and multi-coloured pieces of broken plates.

Simultaneously, the doorbell rang and the brass knocker knocked three times. Startled, he straightened up, let go of the bag and hurried to the door. Looked down: spikey hair, two big eyes atop a small skinny person wielding a plastic box of brushes and cans, and a vacuum cleaner almost as big as her and fit for a wrestle. She saw: a podgy old geezer who needed a shave, drank too much, could have been wearing slippers instead of his blue desert boots.

'Good afternoon! I'm with Catspyjamas. You were expecting me. We spoke on the phone?'

'Uh...That was my brother, actually. Sorry. Please come in. Let me help you with that hoover.'

'Cool. Fanks.'

Henry led the girl into the kitchen.

'Look - There is quite a lot of dust everywhere, but please don't worry about all those figures on the table in the back - they're fragile. I'm afraid the floor's pretty mucky. Upstairs is better. The bookshelves act as a kind of dust magnet, of course - (of course? she puzzled) You do all this yourself?'

'Yeah, like sometimes. We usually work in pairs.' she shrugged 'It's cool. Whassis, is it safe?'- she pointed to the shadows above the table, hung with ancient red draperies and a door-lintel-sized rectangle of sandstone held by ropes to a beam crossing the ceiling.

'Oh, it's nothing much really. I thought years ago, I might do heavy sculpture. Never got round to it. Maybe too much like hard work. See the cut shape down that side? Must have been off the top of a doorway, I guess.' -her face registered incomprehension 'It's perfectly safe. See the beams going down both sides there?' - he pointed to the walls. 'Hey, I'll get out of your way for a while, and let you get on with it.'

'Whatever - gimme a couple of hours or less.' smiling up

Henry got down his leather jacket from the wall hook and headed out again as the girl began unravelling cable from her cleaner.

'See you in a while!' he called to the back of her head.

A meandering wander, XOing the grid of Ladbroke Grove, staring unseeing into the shop and gallery windows. Into Honest Jon's, all round the shop, downstairs and up and back out again, without buying any records. Easy enough: he had enjoyed pop when it meant masturbation fantasies; he grew out of it when he managed to get close to a real girl for the first time. Jazz passed him by; Rachmaninov got through to him but not to the extent that he felt the need to collect the stuff.

The house was lacking something: he could tell as soon as he re-entered. It no longer held a fuggy fragrance of him. A sharp whiff of lemon mixed with the leathery old-boot smell of the floorboards. It was brighter. The windows! They must have been dirty. He couldn't decide if he liked it now. She was tidying up, bustling in yellow rubber gloves. Wiped her forehead with the back of her wrist and said, 'There you go - all done.'
'That's pretty marvellous. Here -' reaching into his hip pocket for his wallet
'I've been paid.'
'You deserve a bonus' -pulling out a twenty
'Thanks. I'll drink that tonight.'
'Oh, yeah, it's Saturday. What's happening?'
'Plenty. This' -flashing a flier from her denim waistcoat pocket - 'in Finchley Road is the one to catch.'

BABY SNAKES Durty Rave & Classic Grave Grooves - MC Flathead

'Wossat? A band?'

'Naoh! Coupla DJs. Good light show, too.'

He saw her out, returned to the kitchen table, sat down. Upstairs to the bedroom, lay down, staring at the ceiling. Sniffed. Lemon...Not I... couldn't settle down anywhere; looked out of the window at the dying day, in a half-trance. He felt uneasy, lying here. It wasn't only because he was no longer sharing the bedroom; it was over a year since he had talked to a estate agent, and he knew he could make a lot of money by moving out to a smaller, one-man-size flat. But he kept putting it off. As he put everything off now. Only the redundancy had freshened things up a little. At seven, he went out to the tandoori place, glad to escape from the strident tang of chemical cleanliness. He walked to Great Western Road for a number 31 northwards to Swiss Cottage. Stopped there in the pub to wash down the remaining miasma of decaying onion, garlic, cumin and chili that clung to his palate. 'Pint of lager please!' 'Stella?' 'Yes, that'll do.'

As he leant on his corner of the bar he became aware of, among the throng, a well-suited young gent with slick-back hair, making elaborate hand-signals to two tarty girls farther round the bar. After a few minutes he realised by the way one of then kept looking his way, that he was being sized up, appraised as a customer, and that he wouldn't do. He wasn't sure. He looked to his left, and right. It was him! He felt... more dismissed than excluded. Not working? Did it show? By a prat like him!

Up Finchley Road and turn left: A huge basement - bigger than it really is maybe - the size defined by the light streaming from one corner, revolving, pulsing as it follows the boom and blast of the bass-heavy music-
Henry lost himself in the sweating crowd. After a few bottles (was it two?) of ice-cold thickly-strong lager (with slices of vegetable matter stuck in the top) he ceased being annoyed by the sideways jostling and almost began enjoying it. Staring directly into the pulsing light beams - a shadow -
'Wey hey, mon capitain!'
'Oh god, Jerry-'
'So what brings you down this 'ole then?'
'Curious...'
'Oh,yeah? Hey - try one a these?'
'Oh I dunno - had a lot to drink already -'
'It's cool, man! They're really mellow.'
A pill so tiny, almost lost in the flashing light. Down it goes, followed by a gulp of bottled Cervesa.

'That's it, man! There you go!'
'Yeah...no doubt...'
Struggling through the dancers towards the
stage again to watch the antics of the VJ. Arm
caught by The Girl.

Dancing in a loose circle

The lights stop moving - the room spins
Duck head: ceiling burps downwards, belching
out from the speakers on the bass beat

She smiles big white encouragement. Is
duck-head cool? Not moving feet.
Two grim guys in dark outfits won't join in.Try
dance with one to wind him up. Bloody
minded, I know. Can't move him. His white
gloves - pushes me; something tingles.

Getting slower. Music getting slower.
Floor rises up - to my knees?

Grab his white glove-hand - force my eyes to
stay open - bit as hard as I can into his fingertip

She push me out of taxi
Key in door

'Wow. It moves.'
'Uhh...what? This your place?'
'Naoh, silly! Look around you. Open your eyes
properly.'
'Oh god...'

Henry was lying face down on the floor, his bed a scattering of cushions from the couch where his feet were propped. He opened one eye fully, gave the linoleum an experimental rub, found a hard breadcrumb between the lino joints; put it in his mouth. Turned his head, looked upwards, The girl sitting, elbows on the table. 'You could have got yourself killed last night, going for those guys like that. Didn't you know who they were?'

'I remember two chaps in black, was it black, kind of grim. One of them went for me.'

'Not the way I saw it. Lucky you got thrown out.'

'Did I?'

'Did I? Yes! And then you started chatting me up!'

'Jeezus. I haven't had a memory blank like this since… a long time ago.'

'Well, I didn't know you were up for pushing big guys around.'

'Neither did I' sitting up, he dragged himself into a seated position on the nakedly saggy, jaggy couch 'Did we…'

'Wot here, on the sofa? No way! I ended up in the bedroom. I fink I deserved that, at least. Couldn't get you up the stairs'

'I remember the taxi at the door… Oh hell, you must have paid.'

'It's cool.'

'…there was something wrong here…'

'You said we were being watched. That's when you smashed these -' lifting old bed sheet to reveal the tiny ruins of six lady sculptures

'Ohh fuck it Ange…'

'Huh?'

'Oh never mind. So we didn't get it on.'

Sadly flashing a tired smirk at his archaic patois. The girl, now standing, arms folded in her skinny sweater, spun away to grab her leather coat, pulling it on.

'Well, I got things to do. Gonna love you and leave you.' backing off towards the corridor. Henry made a half-hearted attempt to follow her, out of politeness, but was glad when she turned the doorlock. He reached out for her other hand and kissed it on the back, offering a vague smile.

'Yeah - loverboy!'

Slam

The tiny room made cavelike by the mattress propped against the window and the light fog of dope-smoke. A heavy roll down on the drums plus a conclusive deep-rippingly jagged chord from the guitar. Nigel threw his guitar down and threw himself into the armchair before the sleepy bass player could get there.

Ringring ringring ringring ringri…

'Aw fack' - reaching to the side, Nigel grabbed the phone, which was on the floor half hidden by sweaters, magazines, bags.

'Wot? Mum? Yeh, yeah, I'm alright. No. Oh, the band? Yeh, funny you calling now. We're playing down Putney on Wednesday... The Niknak. You know that place along from the Half Moon? Yeah. It's like, upstairs. You wanna *see* us? ...No, hah, it's cool. Sure? Okay...Wednesday... about eight.'

Stella put the phone down, clapped her hands and made a happy face at the mirror. Made a point of letting her boy live his own life since he moved out.

Twenty years goes past in my life - it's a blur - but having him, watching him grow, waiting to see what he'd do - it was a lifetime. And now I want to lean on him. It's in the genes, anyway.

Tim Gardner, skinny and eager, seated on the edge of Oscar's little desk, 'So she says she might be promoted to Director of Vision. Whatever that means...'

'The last one was a girl, too. Wanted skyscraper projects and a multi-platform aspect! Fancy forgetting that? I really expected things to change here, but really it's same difference.'

'Multi-platform? Do I see Gary Glitter or Flash Gordon?'

'Hah! Nice one. It's all so much bullshit though.'

'Meaning?'

'Just - well it looks like going to a man. Anyway, we're all going out to get seriously pissed on Wednesday. After Matthew talks to the suits.'

'Wednesday? Night?'

'Yes. Near your end of town - Hammersmith, actually.'

'Good. We haven't had a decent get-together for a good while.'

'There's the production meeting next week-'

'Of course. It's here, in my inner diary' - tapping his head- 'You've been busy though, haven't you?'

'Yes - I was running round like an idiot for a couple of months. It's taking some kind of shape - we really need to nail down our strands, and get the weekends filled first. But it's getting easier - now the indies are calling *me* and begging for commissions. I gave out my mobile number. Can't have them calling me at the Station - that's maybe pushing it a bit.'

'Ha! You mean current affairs and the hard stuff?'

'Well, I've been in contact with film and video people too - London Film Co-op even.

'Well now - that's really my department you know-'

'Surely. But we never really mapped it out-'

'Well now, the arts has always been my area, since radio. Don't forget that.' -he leant forward- 'I should be keeping it up, what with the dumbing-down brigade taking over. Trash was fun while it was ironic-'

'Yes, The Pantie Show!-'

' but it's getting to be the standard. And the tweed jackets are always whining about new media.'

'Yes!' -clapping hands- 'That's it. You've always been the face.' -'I'm more than that. This wouldn't have got off the ground without me' '- But we really need a frontman. A recognisable personality, one to get coverage.'

'Look- Are you seriously suggesting you want me to be some kind of bimbo?'

'Bimbo? Oh no! Really... You know how they are out there. They need personalities-'

'Fuck it, London's getting a new service. That should be enough for coverage anywhere.'

'Well, You know, since the Falklands, news has been big, big news. The IBA figures-'

'Don't tell me about the fucking figures, I took the trouble to actually read them!'

'Did you?'

'Of course I bloody did. It's my job as much as anything.'

'Sorry, I didn't realise you were putting so much time in on this-'

'Right. We agree on that.'

'And, well, at the moment, we're all doing our little bit. I've just been digging around. Doing spadework.'

'Well...I'll keep an open mind about presenting. Just don't forget I practically set this up in the first place.'

'Oh,ho,ho! The forgotten genius..' Oscar looked up abruptly under heavy eyebrows, meeting Tim's eyes

He stood and turned, walked to the window, tapping against the part opened blind, sighed

'How's your end of the floor?'

'Having a bit of a break from real work - I got landed with a bunch of work-experience kids - so I've been showing them the ropes. A couple did media studies or *FT two*, one's made a little film but they don't know a lot about editing or mixing live; even less about plugs and sockets.'
'Well... you can count me in for the pub on Wednesday. I could do with something... mindless. I'll call my better half.'

Just as Stella opened the door to leave the house, the phone rang. 'Damn.' Turned back to pick it up. 'Hello. Oh - Oz-Oscar. Yes, yes. What. Well, that *might* be fun, although I don't always have that much to say to your - Wednesday? Oh, can't come. No. I'm off to see my little boy and his band. Yes. Somewhere in Putney. Oscar. I have to do this. You have your thing, and I may have mine. Look, he's only a kid - give him some room... Yes. And me. Oscar. Yes... Bye.'

At the downstairs bar, too early for the gig, Stella parcelling out her time in sips of vodka and tonic. Nigel barged through the door, guitar in gigbag and dreadlocked blonde underarm -
'Hey- you really came! You're early.'
'I know. I'm just not used to going to gigs.'
'It's cool. We're on first. It was a toss-up between us and The Claim.'
'So The Slakers could be top next time?'
'Yeah! Like, that's the way it goes. Coming up?'

Stella finished her glass and followed the kids up the narrow stair, emerging into a room slightly smaller than the bar-room, a stage at the far end with The Slakers' drum kit and amps set up, while The Claim's kit, half-unpacked, was stacked in front to one side, a lone roadie draped over it, swigging from bottle. The Niknak, previously the pub store-room, had been tarted up in the late Sixties and its walls still bore the sickly purple-and-orange colour scheme of its time. Nigel joined his three fellow Slakers and they began tuning up while his little girlfriend joined two others at the bar. Stella looked round at the girls and managed to draw out a diffident, nervous smile.

The floor there was carpeted, but almost as sticky underfoot as the linoleum-clad standing area.

Nigel plugged in.

'So, who's the lady?' Trevor, sitting behind his Vox organ.

'Me mum.'

'Yore mum? Come on - pull the other one.'

'She's young, ain't she?' Johnson, fiddling with his bass and looking to Sam, drums, who recognised the incipient look of impatient aggression in Nigel and answered with a snare-roll and bass drum/crash cymbal.

Nigel sat on the edge of the stage and played a five-note riff a few times. They were waiting for an audience.

'Boys.' A short, red-faced man in rolled-up shirtsleeves had popped through the doorway. 'We let'em in, in ten minutes. So get ready.'

'We *are* ready.' Nigel got up, stepped on to the stage, went back to his combo and flicked a switch. 'Kinda quiet, innit?'

'Just play, and you'll get your crowd soon enough.'

By the time Stella had bought another vodka it was time to play off. The first number was uncompromisingly loud - a punky thrash, followed by something comparatively sweet and melodic. As Nigel and Johnson were yelling the chorus of the final song in their 45 minute set into their shared mic there was an audience of thirty, who cheered, and some even put their pints on the floor to clap. With the help of a skinny, thin-longhaired and grimly bearded man who had been sitting throughout in the dark corner beside the bar, they were packed up and off-stage in fifteen minutes.

'Nige, are you staying for the other band?' Stella asked

'Uh, don't think so...no - Lucie 'n me, we're off to her place. Anyway, how d'you like the band? Too loud?'

'No! It was fun, really. I liked that slow song you did second. It's time I started catching up with the scene again.'

'But maybe not your speed...'

'Don't forget it was my Stones LP that got you started off, before your first group-

'You listen to The *Stones?*' Trevor's barely disguised deprecation...

'I did, y'know, you like go through changes.' - He was surrounded by reluctant but sagely nodding heads

Stella felt suddenly out of her depth. She had not seen her son for three months, a long time in his life; something in the music had sparked her in a way she had not expected, but she realised she would have to keep her suggestion of a jam session to herself a little longer.

'Mum!' Nigel up close - the others couldn't hear him - 'It was really cool of you to come. Maybe Oscar can get us on the telly. Where is he, then?'

'Drinking with his media pals' Nigel screwing up face - 'Give me a call about your next gig.' Embarrassed but grinning, hugs his mum and turned to join the band, silent and impassive roadie plus girlfriends hustling their luggage through the crowd to the door. What? Over the loud crowd babble and bangs of The Claim setting up

'I'm staying.' Johnson, holding back, his bass in its case. 'I'll have a drink; would you like one?' Stella registered surprise 'Oh, you're driving? But you were drinking voddies?'

'Yes - I mean no. No and yes. I'll have a vodka and tonic, thanks.'

He didn't look any older than her son, but sounded like an adult - his polite self-assurance caught her off balance. They stayed for the end of The Claim's set, only leaving at closing time.

Oscar had wanted her to be his sober driving companion, but she had been through that before: an evening listening to him and his colleagues raving and joking about their world of work, without the blanket of alcohol, was pretty damn intolerable. Come to think of it, it was dreadful enough *with* the alcohol.

Leaving the Niknak, she half-stumbled on the two exit steps outside; as she laughed, Johnson held her arm - she swung round, linking arms. Forgetting for a moment he was a 'kid'.
'Oh thank you! That was close.'
'How are you getting home?'
's'okay - I came on the tube, I leave on the tube.'
They were facing each other. Without thinking she pressed her hand into the small of his back. They drew closer and what he, momentarily unsure of himself, offered as a friendly peck, she immediately segued into a deeply searching interface. He put his hand round the back of her neck, pulled back, sleepy eyed
'I live just a couple of streets back. Like to come back? For a while?'

They walked arm-in-arm; after her eloquent smile nothing more was said. If she had been honest with herself, and had been in the habit of conducting self-analysis on the hoof, she would have admitted that she had come out with no great desire to return. Not even a taxi number in her bag. It began to rain - they walked faster; and quickly arrived at his door. Up stairs, he rested his guitar case and unlocked the door. Inside they had another climb, four storeys to the roof. Johnson threw open the door, laid his case down, half turned to Stella, unsure of what to say next; but he gently held her arm and she pressed closer. She could see the bedroom behind him; boldened by the alcohol and the residue of loud music, and with an awakened sense of liberation from...pretending...she fastened her face again to his and they struggled crab-like, falling on the unmade mattress. Lit only by the upward streetlights on the ceiling, they rolled from side to side, pulling at each other's clothes - but having removed their boots and jeans was far enough. He pushed her down, pulled her knickers to one side and thrust hard against her; as she flinched, he licked his fingers and carefully rubbed into her; at last jamming himself in as his teeth dragged down her neck. Bending tightly, he bit her nipples through her T-shirt as she arched her spine . Her hands ran up his back to his shoulders, gripping hard and down again, nails out all the way and digging into his arse. Behind the sound of their grunting now was the tinny counterpoint of their neck chains rasping against each other. They began to roll from side to side, driven suddenly by her hunger more than his.

She gave one long moan. He sobbed, sobbed.

Four

Henry was beginning to feel that his world was shrinking. He had lost the routine of lecturing / home / work / Shepherd's Bush - without the first, his momentum had seized up and he found it alien to even think about making new works without first getting his life in order. Life being the source. Didn't want to see Jerry again. Didn't want to see Ozzie again. Ozzie fucking invaded this home. It was fine as it was. A bit smelly, all right. But it's fucked now. It's not my home. It doesn't smell right.

Hot bath. Soak in it. Pick at the chipped enamel. Ow. It's under my nail. Soak a little more.

Out. Need a shave.

Razor smells pongy.

Jesus fucking Christ, the bags under my eyes.

Kitchen. Eat crunchy stuff. Some yoghurt left. Peach flavour.

Where's my socks?

Stella refused Johnson's offer of morning (instant) coffee and headed straight to the tube, not sure whether to feel liberated or confused. He leant well out of the window to watch her go down the street. But saw only the waving treetops. He felt for his neck chain, found it was missing, broken. 'Fuck.' Thought about it as he looked round and up towards the lightening sky, his feet kicking against the wall as he rested on his elbows. The germ of a song...

Outwards plodded the aged potter on his westend way. Henry had a half-baked plan to wander round the galleries; always a good ploy when he was out of ideas for work, or just putting off starting. He was well past the time when he might have found something to stimulate him there though; he had his own thing going (when it was going) and the choice in the big galleries was between anally-retentive realism and mixed-media conceptualism. He had meant to get the 15 bus in Westbourne Park Road, but got there just in time to see the back end of same, so started walking.

Past the dead cinemas on Chepstow Road and at the bottom end of Queensway. The tiny shop across from Paddington Station, selling telescopes, knives, watches. The equally personal old shop hidden behind Edgware Tube Station containing bakelite radio knobs and obsolete valves. He was just old enough to feel an affinity with the blokes who had spent their lives running these little emporia, stocking and selling things that interested them; things whose only common denominator was their value as perceived by the man behind the counter.

He had crossed 'Old' Marylebone Road and wandered as far as Crawford Street, which as always, got him thinking about leggy supermodels, when it occurred to him that hanging round the west end galleries when he should be sculpting or, even better, getting drunk with famous mediastars in the Groucho Club may not look to the world like the behaviour of a successful artist. He stopped at the pub in Crawford Street, because it was there. Too early today for a beer - eleven-thirty; and maybe a stiffener was too much. They had coffee's on the blackboard. He decided to ignore the syntax and try one. It was tolerable, if a little weak, and he washed down a packet of nuts before taking a piss and heading back to the southwest.

In Chiswick, Stella found a note stuck to the fridge door:

'where did you end up last night? call me'

-She thought about this for a while.

'Hello? May I speak to Oscar Early please?'

'Yes. May I ask who is speaking?'

'Stella Nelson.'

'Thank you. Please hold the line.'

'Stella! Well now - where on earth did you get to last night?'

'Oh, one of Nigel's pals put me up.'

'Why didn't you call me?'

'What for? You were out, anyway.'

'You could have left a message.'

'I'm sorry.'

'Yes, you could have been anywhere.'

'...Damn! I'm not sorry! Why should I be? I could have been anywhere, anywhere I liked, you shouldn't care, and it makes no Difference to you.'

'What the hell kind of a way is that to talk? You...'

Stella had cut him off. The old hippy in her had suddenly morphed into a mature and self-interested adult, twenty years late. She felt a little shaky; her heart rate had gone up; her sweat glands opened and wafted upwards the musky remnants of the night.

Oscar threw the phone down, strode angrily out of his little room to the water-cooler. It was bloody warm again.

Henry had never liked walking that much away from his usual haunts; he was accustomed to getting round by Tube, or on the surface of the city, by car. It was a surprise to find how soon he could get to Kensington. There was nothing about Park Lane, or even the more densely crowded Knightsbridge, to keep him lingering. The pavement as he moved on looked, in its varied face, occasionally extra-familiar, the slate conjuring up childhood intimacy, that closeness to the ground, playing games on it; the gridly textured concrete suggesting...the unfamiliar...or something to do with making things. Just for a moment he looked up and saw himself reflected in the shop window, superimposed on elegantly straining and perfectly sculpted ladies in lingerie, frozen in mid-prance. He was slouching, like a little old wino, a lost soul, while other shapes broke from the multitude and darkly sliced across the glass. He lingered not. Straightened up. Strode onwards.

Brompton Road; turned off at Pelham Crescent and deliberately explored the back streets, meandering westwards, he imagined, like 'taking a line for a walk', as he circled round The Boltons and looked up at the thinning leaves in the central slit-shaped garden. Again, he began thinking about existence.

Angela can't see these trees. But she doesn't care. I wouldn't, either. It's between me and the leaves. If I leave...

Yesterday this 'me' did not exist as the experience of these trees was to come. Now this 'me' exists - one who experiences trees.

Tonight this 'me' will be dead. In twenty or thirty years there will be no more 'me's.

It doesn't matter.

The white stucco and little gardens cast him out into the company of Redcliffe Gardens - he had had a vague plan to head for the pubs of Earls Court Road to ponder quietly about his awakening feeling of concord with mortality, but something about Brompton Cemetery attracted him; he followed the railings round to the gate and entered. A good place to gather your thoughts. Never thought of them that way until he met that mad Scot from Glasgow, funny chap, quite old but talked about pop music like a kid. One of Parkin's customers...

Well away from the central path and among the less well-attended old gravestones, he sat down on a mossy lid, leant back on his hands, sighed deeply. Looked back out towards the traffic and people beyond the wall, his mind empty.

'Hey look pal, have a slug a this?'

For a second Henry thought it was the Scot.

'Oh, Christ, I didn't see you there. What's that?'

'Only Four Crown, see, wire in, go on.'

'You must be Scottish.'

'Aye, fae a long time ago! Goan, help yersel.'

Henry reluctantly taking the sticky bottle and gulping a little gulp. It went down too fast for him to savour the sugary taste but left a bitterness on the back of his tongue. Handed it back; his new companion wrinkled in a warm smile; he seemed pleased to have found someone to share his bottle. He began looking round him expectantly. 'I'm waitin' for a very special lady here. You're maybe waitin' for something too?

'No, I...'

'Well you never know what ye might find in life, just hangin' about, know what I mean.'

'I'm not really just hanging about. I'm - taking a break.'

'...Aye, that's the way, tak a break.'

The traffic continued its quiet surge outside the wall. The drinker leaned his arse against the stone tabletop edifice, his head back, closing his eyes, almost beatifically.

It was beginning to darken, the leafy trees melding into silhouettes, as a blonde woman in a knobbly charity-shop coat appeared from behind them.

'Hey, darlin! How're ye <u>doin</u>?' -eyes opening, the bottle lowered

Henry appraised her broad mouth, tired-bright eyes and grubby hair as she replied, her face inclined and quizzically turned, in a soft and husky voice, 'I'm doing all right, baby. And I won't be back. Ciao.'

She straightened up and walked away, purposefully, towards the gate.

'Fuck me. Never even said goodbye. Heh!'

Something about her... Henry watched her until she had become one with the crepuscular far end of the cemetery, then turned back to the mystery Scot. He wasn't there, either.

Stella had lost touch with her old pals on the music scene, but she was vaguely aware that several of them had drifted out of it; some taking their day-jobs seriously as they had not done before, some taking their drink more religiously than ever. And one or two having completely given up all activity. She remembered how Nico had a brief return to the bright lights when she teamed up with a punk band somewhere up north. Miles Davis was always finding kids to join his band, no matter how old he got, and so he kept up. Or kept ahead, some of the guys used to insist. Why shouldn't girls do it, too?

Nigel heard about a vacant gig - the band due to play: The Motels, had fragmented after their drummer began moonlighting with another band, and their guitarist passed it on as they stood side by side, making eyeball love to the shiny newbodied guitars in a Denmark Street shop window. He told his mother, half-hoping the choice of venue would put her off:
'It's, y'know, the Hotel, but like in the basement.'
'Oh yes, now I know what you're talking about. Not the tea-room. Downstairs. Those narrow stairs.'

'You've been there?!'

'Nige, I sung there. You were tiny then.'

The décor was probably just as sordid as it was when Stella had last seen it, although the dim blue light made it difficult to be sure. The sweaty basement was full of second-generation Goths. A girl, her eyes painted with batwings, stood alone in the spotlight, ululating hoarse slap-bang rhythms which carried words in a near monotone, while her male guitarist kept up a meandering backdrop on his Rickenbecker 12-string copy, sitting well away in the shadows, in the audience. Then The Slakers plugged in.

In the cramped room, full of bodies, a low decibel count was enough to change the pressure - the crowd moved back from the PA except for one determined headbanger, dirty blond dreadlocks flying as he threw himself around a mere arm's length from the speakers. Stella retreated towards the bottom of the stairs. When the set was over and another drumless act was moving into the band corner, she was glad to see the boys packing up. They followed her up to the street and waited while their roadie went for his van.

'Mum, was it like that when you played here?'

'No, Nige. It was pretty dirty in those days, but maybe a little more wholesome. I'm sure we didn't play so loud.'

'Ha ha!'

Their gear was on the pavement; Sam, with blonde Lucie came out of the door with the last pieces of drum kit: she with the bass pedal and he with the cymbals in their box. 'Oi, Nige, how about Young's?'

'Yeah! I could do that.'

'What about those Goths, then?'

'Yeah, livin in the past!' - Trevor added

The van came back and they gratefully loaded their gear and themselves into the back as the rain began to fall. Johnson and Stella both managed to get the seat, beside the roadie. As they drove away, Johnson said, 'Wiz - what do you say to one in Young's, before dumping the stuff?'

'Now you're talkin, boy. I've got some thirst after that hole.' Wiz took them straight to a well-lit lane beside the pub, where he could park.

After two, or maybe three pints had passed, Stella in the noise and exhilaration of the moment, made that suggestion after all. Within the hearing of Nigel and Sam she said, 'I've been thinking seriously about singing again. Maybe I could work with a band like you boys.'

'Really? Seriously?'

'Yeah. You know there's no boundaries these days. Punk, funk or jazz. World music...'

'World music, what the fuck's that? Means fuckall,' interrupted Sam

Lucie was listening - pulled herself out from under Nigel's arm and brushed back her hair- 'It's nice. I heard it on Radio Three...'

'Just a name. They can't play a back beat, most of em.'

Wiz sat and watched, relaxed and calm as he rolled another one and sipped his Guinness. Trevor and Johnson returned from the bar to their table. 'What's up Sam?' asked Trevor.

'World music. Just bloody hippy junk.'

'No, it's Mum, talking about gigging...'

'I've been thinking about it for ages. Once you get it in the blood, you never really leave it.'

'I can *see* it. You should get up there - else you'll regret it.' said Wiz, expelling a cloud of Gold Leaf

'I could... even do some numbers with you kids.'

The boys were embarrassed, as she was afraid they would be- 'd'you remember Nico did those gigs with that band up north, after everyone had forgotten her?'

'Nico?' Sam sounded mollified, although Johnson surprised the rest of them by admitting, eyebrow raised, 'It sounds interesting; could be worth trying.' Mentioning Nico swung the vote in her favour. At first she was surprised to see these boys so taken with the German's reputation - then she forced herself to look properly at Nigel's little blonde girlfriend. Apart from the dreadlocks...

Life in Chiswick, chez Early, had been a matter of impersonating the successful couple instead of being one. As Oscar's name and earning capability grew, so his insecurity and blustering ego grew. Stella was as impressed by his charm as she was by his growing ring of admirers, enough to allow herself to be persuaded to move out to the thespian suburbs, and enough to allow herself to be removed stealthily from her own ill-paid but fulfilling career. Neither of them was really aware of the gradual change in their life together. She was a frustrated singer, who depended on him and his friends for companionship, having lost touch with so much of her own life; but increasingly she found she had little in common with these people. Her days were getting too long: her boy had left the nest, and the new house was more or less decorated and fixed up. A period as part-time librarian at the local library, followed by an unpaid job 'facilitating' interest in music at the secondary school were hardly enough to fulfil her life. She resented being where she was and associated Oscar with her frustration - so he represented failure to her. He was driven by a determination to succeed where his father (whom he hated, and unconsciously impersonated) had failed. She was ideal for him: sexy and charismatic - they wouldn't ordinarily have met if it hadn't been for that TV show, and lucky that he had only taken it over for two weeks. It all worked well for a few years, but it seemed to be going wrong. She didn't do charisma in close-up, of course, but sexy… she didn't seem to care about being his sex doll any more. Surely, they fucked occasionally, and she had orgasms, but not noisy ones like they used to be. She just seemed quietly pleased like someone who had completed a task.

A rare evening together: she perched on the couch; still used the little fold-out picnic table but he, sitting in the armchair, preferred a tray on his knees. They ate their tortellini-with-salami, and watched a film on TV.
'She's like that girl who used to be joined to wosname.'
'who, her?'
'No, her, the blonde. With the blue eyes.'
'Who?'
'Who what?'
'Joined to who?'
'Yes, that's what I'm saying.'
…
'Paul Newman!'
'Paul…I used to wear stuff like that, you know.'
'That bloody woman who's taking over Current Events talks like that.'
'And it went with the act.'
'Act? Yeah that was a good show. And it looked good on the box. I should get something like that set up again.'
'I don't think my voice will have lost much in a couple of years'

'Trouble is the demarcation between arts and ents'

'I could even write. My piano - I should get it fixed'

'We can only make things better with a new station, I hope'

'No, it's better to get a new...'

'It's top-heavy with business, is the problem'

'...piano'

'I should care less - I won't be there in months.'

'I always liked the Wurlitzer sound. It's sharp.'

'All being taken over by bloody accountants, everywhere. In Europe it's different.'

'It's okay for just one voice...'

'I've told them so but it just doesn't sink in.'

When they talked, she believed they were talking about music and about her; he believed they were talking about him and his work. In reality, they talked about what was on the telly. In the papers.

At the bottom of the steps, Stella stepping out of Ladbroke Grove Tube. 'The GBH. That was a good gig. I could do one like that again. To start. God, the other pub's changed names again. That was good, too. Then they had punk. Then...it got quiet...'

Round the corner into Cambridge Gardens. She had phoned first:

'Ello. Morgan Rush Promos.'

'O hello, it's Stella Nelson here. Is Morgan there please?'

'Morgan. O I'm sorry dear, he's retired from the business. It's still his company, though. May I help? Sorry, wossat name again?'

'Nelson. Stella Nelson. Well that's quite a surprise. Retired? We did lots of business.'

'Did you an all? You wif a company?'

'No I - I'm a singer. I've had a break from gigging, and I'd like to get some bookings again.'

'You got a band, then?'

'Yes. Yes, of course.'

'I'm just looking for your name here... Oh. Yes. Jazz. We're really concentrating on rock these days... O yeah I see, you've been in the book, well back in the day.'

'Yes that's right. A few years.'

'Hey, you playing anywhere?'

'Yes, we've a few gigs dotted about.'

'Dotted...Round here, like?'

'Yes, the pub in Golborne Road.'

'Well that's cool, if it's the one I think, but no money. Live round here, then?'

'No. used to - but - I could drop in...'

'Drop in. Like, when? Where you calling from?'

'The west. Chiswick.'

'Welll, maybe not this week - not sure...'

'Maybe another time-

'No, hey, it's cool. Could you make it, like, the next few days?'

'Well, how about tomorrow?'

'Yeah! Tomorrow's okay! I'm not able to make any promises of course, not yet. But we could look at it. Say, maybe two?'
'Two o'clock. I'll be there.'

She had expected a phone call might open up old friendships and even lead to getting a clutch of decent gigs for the still formative new band; hardly prepared for this burst of acceleration - but she found the basement - the whole building looked dingier than she remembered: the paint was flaking off and moss was gathering in the cracks. One thing unchanged: the discreetly tiny red plastic sign by the door with MR Promos cut into it in white. Having carefully descended, hoping to avoid scraping her heels on the step risers, she leant straight to the doorbell, finger first. It gave way, softly, as if it, too, were moss. No sound that she could detect. A few seconds. Knocked, tatum tatum.

After a few moments, the door opened: a fair-haired 'boy' of about twenty-five looked out.
'Oh, hello. You must be...'
'Stella'

'Stella. I'm Brian.' 'Brian…' 'You called yesterday, yeah. Come in, please' He turned back, held the door open and she stepped over the little mud-grid to the red lino of the short, ill-lit hallway. The back door, half-open, held an ambience, rather than a smell, of kitchen. Into the little office through the door on the right. In the office all the walls were painted red. A huge planning calendar and jokeshop gold record on the wall with several vintage posters - Be Stiff, Bob Kerr and his Whoopee Band at the Golden Lion, Screamin' Lord Sutch, Ten Years After: Railway Hotel. Her host leaped in and threw himself into the seat behind the little desk, which almost colour-matched his crumpled shiny grey suit.

'Please! Have a seat! We're a bit low on hospitality this mor- today - girl Friday's off. Well off!'

'Thanks.' -she lowered herself into the 'butterfly' chair- 'I remember this chair from way back. Heal's, it must have been. Morgan was going to get rid of it.'

'He did! But I brought it back - thought it had some class.'

'He said people couldn't get back out of it, and it was hard enough to get rid of them to start with sometimes.'

'Hah! You know the old man pretty well, then?'

'Old? Oh, he's your dad?'

'Well - Yeah, chair was in my room for a bit. So! You're up for a few gigs? I can definitely get you two dates round at the KPH, plus a couple out at East Sheen. For a start.'

'Oh that - that's a good start. You didn't sound so enthusiastic yesterday...'

'Well, I've been checking up on you! And the gigs, too. I did say that we've been concentrating on rock, as far as live gigs go. If you say you're jazz, right away you're limiting yourself to one or two kind of venues-'

'I didn't mention jazz.'

'Didn't you?'

'No. I used to sing with a combo or a piano. But I've joined with a younger bunch-'

'Oh, really?'

'-and we're mixing a few kinds of music together. I don't know what you could call it.'

'Well! What do <u>you</u> call it?'

Chalice From The Palace was named by Nigel after an afternoon of combined frustrated efforts to combine words into memorable shapes. A final joint had been passed round, the last can of lager had gone down. 'This is doing my head in man,' said Sam.

Nigel coughed on the joint and passed it on, saying in a thin voice, 'How about Chalice?'

'Chalice? People'll expect rasta stylee,' said Sam.

'From the Palace,' added Nigel.

'Chalice from the Palace?' said Stella.

'Yeah!' Nigel looked round at the others, 'It was a film, on telly, at Christmas. The chalice from the palace has the brew that is true.'

They got mixed receptions at their first public appearances, in pubs where music was treated as wallpaper by most of the customers. Those who had expected their usual fare of easy listening retreated to other parts of the bar, or shouted louder and drank more heavily (which raised the band's status with the management) but there were enough within hearing range who were beyond keeping their musical appreciation categorised - some dance-like shuffling even took place.

Stella and Oscar continued to live together as the Famous Couple, although their sex-life, an engine with no oil, ground to a halt. He was increasingly centred on setting up a small independent TV company with his unhappy fellow-workers (in deadly open secret), while she, as well as rediscovering her stage legs, was also enjoying fucking as she had not done since she was in her twenties. For a short few months it had fed back into her relationship with Oscar, but she very nearly destroyed everything by almost saying that name she had in a very short time become accustomed to using, in a mock-polite tone, in ecstasy.

'Johnson! Did you two write these songs? You saying <u>you</u> wrote them?' asked Nigel as they set up their gear to rehearse, in the Sea Scout Hall

'Yeah, sure we did. She had these words. And some chords.'

'I thought she-'

'We like, collaborated.'

'When?'

'When what?'-the four continued clattering, dragging, drum kit and speakers- a cat appeared from behind a dusty dark velvet curtain and scuttled away again into the kitchen- 'When did you just, like, collaborate?'

'Any time. She comes over to my place. What's it to you, we done the job.'

'You done the job! It matters a fucking lot to me!''

'Well, you can write a song, too.'

'I don't mean that - I...' drumstick flying between the two- 'Hey, wot the fuck's got into you two?' asked Sam, 'Stella'll be here in five. I wanna do that thrash thing first.'

Although The Slakers continued their struggle against obscurity, sharing the rounds of London's little gigs with an ever-changing panoply of other lesser-knowns, they doubled easily enough as a kind of backing band; quietly hoping that this would be the connection that might bring fame and riches. Stella had lost a few notes at the top since she retired, she was out of practice at hitting and holding the ones in the middle and her tone was throaty and rough; probably the cigarettes; so she settled for a theatrical half-talk, as she remembered from ancient Noel Coward records - but she tried adding a little more passion. From the boys' point of view, her presence carried it.

Their first rehearsals had been awkward: Sam and Trevor were unsure whether to use her first name, but she broke the ice when Trevor asked, 'E, m...what kind of speed is this meant to be? I can't tell from the words...'

'Trev. Stella's the name. (she felt uncommonly in control, for once) We're going to be on the one stage, and facing the animals together.'

Trevor nearly said 'whatever' but thought better and relaxed.

Nigel felt awkward, too, but for another reason. He had hardly seen his mother for two, long years, but she *was* his mother, and now he had to share her with strangers who were going to treat her as a mate. She had changed, too: she no longer spoke to him, adult to child, but almost as an equal. Sometimes, when he was growing up, he had felt older than her - but he saw this as being her fault for being uncool.

She would always feel guilty and regretful about his leaving - regretful at losing him to keep Oscar. The new man in her life saw her little boy as a rival - who had not long before grown out of sharing his mother's bed - regularly exploding into anger with him over slight differences, to Nigel's deep and resentful bewilderment. Stella buried her resentfulness towards Oscar, and felt guilty at her feeling of relief when Nigel left, as she had had to worry about getting him looked after when she had gigs; and then admitting that he was growing up and could look after himself, she was free of worry about his partying, his adolescent free-living when she was unable to keep watch over him. She knew he had plenty of the 'wrong kind' of role models in her own circle.

Trevor reported, at the next rehearsal, that he had heard of a possible gig in Camden. They were sitting on old packing cases in the half-abandoned shop two streets from their garage store, arguing about an intro. He managed to break into the debate - 'Ere, Sam, that slow stuff - with the ride - sounds like The End.'

'Whadda ya mean, the end, you fucker?'

'Haha! No! The band, I mean. Not remember them at The Border?'

'O yeah, they done a CD,' said Nigel

'Well anyway, I saw them at the warehouse thing couple of weeks back, Brixton - '

'Yeah saw the poster'

'And you missed out - called something like koolpix.' -'Koolpox?' -'There's gonna be another one in Camden.'

'Not a bad name...' - Johnson mused

'Another what?' Stella asked

'I dunno what you'd call it. Like a club, but it's art and... shit. And some music. I got the phone number for Camden from a girl.'

Nigel laughed: 'A girl! That's better! Fuckin time you got one, too.'

'Ooh, well, her boyfriend was there. No way.'

'Hey,' said Sam, 'Joe Strummer says it's cool to steal'em. It was in the NME.'

'-like the ones you pick up? I seen em. That one in 'oxton, man!'

'What the fuck was up with her?'

'Like that chick outside the chemist...'

'The chemist? That orrible blonde I seen her.'

Trevor spoke up

'Whoa man I spoke to her too an all - hey, *shut up Nige* - an she's like, 'Got any amps?' and I'm like, 'Yeah, a Marshall hundred!'

It looked like being their biggest crowd yet. An empty warehouse on the Grand Union Canal, squatted by a tribe of artists for the three-day event. No money; but the glory could be adequate compensation. It was a worrying experience for Stella: she had missed out on the post-punk multi-media circus scene. She was unaware that the 'scene' as such, did not exist - the participants were making it up as they went along. It took her back to those telescoped months in 1967 when jazz, rock, drugs, Dressing Up and light shows collided orgiastically, nearby in the Roundhouse, or down in Soho. The boys were quite jumpy and excited, although when their turn came there had been no fanfare. They walked on to the improvised stage, with, above, a partly dressed girl dancer spinning and twisting around a rope from the roof to one side, and a painter dressed in second-hand evening suit, throwing red and green stuff at white boards to the other; getting half of the paint on himself.

But Chalice From The Palace drew a little crowd, as their volume announced their presence to the whole warehouse. And the louche atmosphere allowed Stella to let go as she couldn't remember ever having done before - the band responded by casting aside their 'grown-up' pretensions and playing more like The Slakers at full clumsy tilt. Having run out of songs as the Chalices, they had to morph back into The Slakers for an encore. Nigel shouted the lines, and Stella repeated them in some kind of improvised tune.

They tumbled off the back of the riser, as their ever watchful roadie began shifting some of their gear. Sam jumped on Trevor's back, legs crossing round his waist - they both fell to the concrete floor as Nigel, painfully happy, hugged his mother and Johnson stood awkwardly back. Sam separating himself from the dis-organist, shouted, 'Yahoo!'

Johnson turned back , 'Wiz - we can't leave this lying here now - better get it back to the van then?'

'I'm doin that very thing ma boy. (smiling) Of course I'd appreciate a helping hand.'

They managed between them to get the drums and back-line out and packed away in fifteen minutes; the PA was laid on by the squatters. As they worked, the rest of the group wandered through the warehouse, relaxing and enjoying the other performers and wanderers. Sam went straight to a cheap hippy beer stall, got a Grolsch and carefully downed it in one. Immediately, the three turned back for three more beers, which they began drinking gratefully, but more gently.

Johnson reappeared, Wiz behind him. Both gulping Carlsberg Specials, which Wiz had packed for the occasion. 'Nigel! What d'you say we keep that one like that?'

'Wo? Shouting too?'

'Yeah! The shouting an all!' -Sam yukked

'Fuck me - it was all fucking great. We aught to be fucking rich.'

Stella could not remember the last time she had felt so uncomplicatedly happy. The after-gig glow, the unreal punky fairground surroundings, just watching the boys letting it all hang out and forgetting about all the boring stuff...

After midnight, she and Johnson began holding back, letting the gang go ahead, passing a row of dark and lumpy oil paintings, crudely stuck into old gold frames and hanging in the concrete shadows. When everyone's attention was on the stand-up comedian with the leg-shagging dog, they sneaked out of the side door into the street, to find a taxi.

Five

Henry had decided to escape to what was left of his childhood. Outside the cemetery, he walked to North End Road and found a southbound black cab.

'Where to, mate?'

'Borough, please. The High Street.'

'Borough?' -'Yes.' -'That'll take us a bit, at this hour.' -'That's okay. I've got the time.'

He sat back and enjoyed the journey down, along Chelsea Embankment, over Vauxhall Bridge and by a tortuous backstreet route missing Elephant & Castle.

'Here we are mate, the High Street.'

'Yes, just here'll do, by the pub.'

'Can't stop 'ere, have to go round the corner, all right.'

'All right.'

He paid up, got out and looked up at Marshalsea Road. It seemed cleaner than he remembered.

Everything's been bloody cleaned up.

Back to the pub. Outside, it looked welcomingly shabby. Warm indoors. He caught the barman's eyes immediately, over the heads of three established drinkers in suits. A pint of Guinness. And a whisky. Never used to drink whisky much. It was Ozzie, after the Glasgow job, started buying them, little brat. Good in the winter. Decent pub, this. I like standing at the bar. No room to sit, anyway. Don't know what I'll do later. Don't care. I'm running out of money. I hate dealing with that business at the Job Centre and the Tax People. Another Guinness.

When one of the high stools became vacant, he had taken it over. By the time they were calling Last Orders his forehead was almost propped on the edge of his glass. He straightened himself, swilled the dregs of his final Guinness round the bottom of the glass, drank them down and carefully lowered himself to the floor. The Gents' was easy enough to find - the two-way traffic had increased as the light took on that warm, mushy glow. It was well flooded near the pisser, so he took a sharp left turn to the cubicle, thereby avoiding damage to his blue suedes.

In the street he stood for a while in thought. He didn't really feel like going back to the Grove - it felt invaded and he couldn't think there. Too late to find a B&B though, if there were any. And everyone he knew here was living somewhere else now. He walked very slowly towards the tube station. To his left, the brightly coloured roaring streak of traffic. To the right: the comforting presence of ancient red brick. Coming towards him was a strange-looking fellow - quite tall, long carefully unkempt dark hair, huge beard, in a broad-shouldered suit of something pale and shiny, that looked one size bigger again. Henry began a swerve to avoid, but the big guy turned,too.

'Hey man, I seen you before. You from here?'

'No. Yes. I grew up here. Live in the west now.'

'Where?'

'Ladbroke Gro…'

'Ladbroke Grove! Man I *love* that place. It's special in many ways. You made the right move, man! So how d'you like the Borough?'

Henry couldn't ignore the feeling that he was being manipulated, but an evening on the booze plus the deeply-felt need to talk to someone - anyone, allowed him to shut down the part of himself that would normally have reacted with a 'fuck-off'.

'It's - oh I don't know, really, haven't had a good look round here for years. It's been cleaned up a bit. I take it you must be local?'

'Yeaah! I'm local for sure, All my scene, too. Hey, stick around - you got the time?' his face beaming with a magnanimous smile

'No, I reckon I'll come back maybe tomorrow and get a proper look.'

By now they were walking side by side, Henry weaving slightly and the other looking round and back to him.

'Good place to stay here if you wanna change - be a tourist.'

Henry suddenly had the feeling that this white kid, bearded up and besuited to resemble an oil sheikh, was propositioning him

'Oh, not for me, really…'

'I got a little B n' B here.'

'What, you mean for the night? I don't know…'

'Hey my friend, I'll show you. And you're a native, you can find what you want from there.'

The stranger had a persuasively gentle but firm way of suggesting. Probably the last time Henry had been spoken to like this was by his mother. They turned down a few side streets until they were at a post-war tenement, concrete and brick with just one entrance at one end of the building. Henry had an increasing feeling of foreboding but decided to ignore it as merely the fear of the unknown.

'See? I got rooms here. Plenty room. One for you. Come in, have a look.'

'Not sure if I got the cash..' (he bluffed)

'No problem! You can try this room, gratis. It's only just gone empty, you can use it, it's no sweat. Come and see if you like it.'

'I might come back, see you tomorrow-'

'Heyy man. You're here. Just have a look see.'

'Well... I remember playing round here...' he added to the back of the big kid's head '... I'll have a look.'

Up the stairs and through the door on the top landing to the corridor. The sound of children shouting mixed with bassy music thumps. Smell of rancid butter and disinfectant. They stopped on the first landing upwards and Henry's new friend walked through the double doors. A door opened; low voices. He strained to see through the mottled glass windows in the doors, then jumped backwards, startled, as his host reappeared with a young West Indian woman, big eyes, cropped hair, white blouse, leather jeans. She held a huge bunch of keys, smiled a sleepy smile for Henry. He liked the smile, although he couldn't tell whether it was tired or stoned.

'Meet... my woman. Most perfect girl in the world. Give him the keys, baby.' She stood away in time to avoid a slap on her arse and gave Henry the keys. He could now see she was quite tired and maybe unhappy about being called "baby". Beardie's arm round his shoulders. Steered away again to the stairwell and up to the next floor. In the corridor he surrendered the keys to their owner who with much jangling opened the first door, throwing it back.

'There you go, man! Perfect for the man about town.'

It was a single room, entered through a tiny space with bathroom off to one side and kitchen to the other. A single junkshop bed, chair and table. The remains of straw matting on the floor.

(Jesus Christ!) 'It - It's rather basic...'

'It's yours. You can stay here tonight. If you like it, you can move in. Talk to me tomorrow. Look. I *trust* you. Here's the keys.'

'Oh I don't know...'

A look blackly offended, danger in the eyes - his eyelids lowered

'Well - I guess, all right. What about the keys tomorrow?'

'Come see me, room five, the floor below. Any time after eight.' Patting his chest -'I'm Richard.'

'Henry.'

'Henry, it's good to know you. Have a good rest. Café round the corner to the right's open late, if you want... So-' he leaned back, hands on hips- 'You want a girl? I can get you one. Twenty minutes, easy.'

'Huh! I really couldn't-'

'No?' Henry held up his hand insistently- 'Oh. That's too bad. I know one or two, young. New. Think about it'

'I'm in no state, look-'

'Okay. Forget it. Tomorrow.' Richard turned, head down, and left.

After a moment looking out to the dullness of the passageway Henry pushed the door shut, felt in his jacket pocket for cigarettes. A couple Benson and Hedges left. He lit up, sucked the smoke down deep and gently breathed out as he looked out of the window for a while. Explored the kitchen and found a glass, cleaned out the grime, put it down. Turned on the tap again, into his opened mouth and had a rudimentary mouthwash. He wiped the dust from the mirror above the bathroom sink, looked at his face for a moment. Realised he was really drunk, and how obviously he must have been to others. He stuck his hand under the Hot tap, ran the water - somewhere a heater clicked on, but the water remained stubbornly cold. One last leak in the brown-stained toilet bowl, then he switched off the dim light and lay down fully-clothed, his jacket collar pulled up, on the creaky bed. He lay there for a while, staring at the orange street light slanted across the ceiling; terrified that sleep might never come.

Stella lying on her face. She drifted awake.

The bed smells of him: smelly feet and cheap aftershave - and something else, like butter or cocoa. His skin...I can see him in the dark against the crumpled white sheet. On his back, his neck stretched out and his head off the edge of the mattress, almost touching the floor. I can't hear him breath. (Ozzie snores sometimes, even with his mouth shut.) My hand, gently on his tummy flat, stretched out the hip bone thigh curly hair his little joystick sleepy not so little though...it woke up, its head looking up
'Unngh'
he didn't wake but he moved his arm from his chest. lift it - a little squeeze - it's bigger, and hard again.
climb over, gently fit round it, I arch my back it rubs my button... yes
- he's sitting up - head between my breasts. licking up to my neck. smell his hair. baby. rub harder. hold me. throws me back. deeper like that ooh it's so good like that... slow...
angry
hungry
yes

Oscar had been so deeply concerned with setting up in business as a slightly clandestine team member in the new independent TV company while keeping his contracted work running at the Station that he had neglected the home life - eating at work, coming home late just to sleep, wash and breakfast. Stella decided not to insist that he took an interest in her rebirth as a performer; he had, after all, talked her out of performing in the first place - and she didn't feel as if she could handle his knowing about Johnson.

Sometimes, though, Wiz would drop her off home well after midnight, when Oscar had already settled down for the night. She would either still be buzzing with adrenalin from the gig, or mildly stoned. 'Stella? Wossatime?'

'Oh I dunno. One, I think.'

'Christ, not again. I really could do with a good sleep, <u>you know</u>.'

Over breakfast one morning they agreed to cease sharing a bed - Oscar moved to the single bed in the spare room. He was nursing his anger of the previous disturbed night when he suggested this, and was surprised - relieved, but a little offended, when Stella readily agreed.

For one long weekend he was in Paris for an international media festival, ostensibly for the Station, but he hoped to collect new contacts for his own yet unborn company. She had already been getting relaxed about seeing Johnson without the excuse of playing gigs, just phoning him to visit his flat for some 'songwriting' which was as much about smoking a few joints and rolling on the mattress as anything. Making up always-new stories to cover all-nighters was getting more difficult; but it hardly seemed to matter as Oscar had dropped his bossy manner and rarely asked. As far as he was concerned, she had become a lot quieter, made less demands and seemed to know her place. He had liked her as she was when they met: sexy with no *ideas*. He hadn't expected her to start getting stroppy, making demands.

Monday night was strictly for unknown bands. Although Chalice From The Palace were getting a little reputation among nouveau hipsters, they were far from being a Name; but playing the little black cavern in Soho was better than 'paying to play'. After the first song, a drunk in the crowd of twenty began shouting out a request for '96 Tears', a song from the Slakers' repertoire. They thought at first he was joking, but after he had repeated his request several times between numbers, and as the club had no bouncers, they agreed without consultation to run each song into the next without pause. The result was close to the spirit of punk - but cool, as Stella leant down over the edge of the stage to deliver her lines. Finishing early, they were doing their get-out as the other band plugged in. Wiz, looking wizened as ever, said it as he ran two wheeled combos out the back together: 'Coolpunk! Yeahh!'

The drive back took in all band members' homes and would logically have dropped Nigel first, but he insisted on staying on for the ride. 'sokay - I'll get the tube. Just wanna stay out late.' The rest of the band except for Johnson looked at him as if he was a fool. Johnson suspected otherwise. And when they had parked in his street, he, and Stella, found themselves unable to suddenly be honest with Nigel. Johnson got out, and she was fidgeting to get ready to follow him when Nigel got out first.

'Look man! Is this? I *thought* - is she stopping here?'

'Well, yes... you know... we get together...'

'Together! You and her!'

'You knew that. The songs...'

'She's my *mum*, you cunt!' Nigel thumping Johnson hard on the chest

Stella and Wiz both jumped out - she wanted to reassure her son but Wiz grabbed the two by their shoulders and separated them as if the bassist, standing Christlike with his arms outstretched was about to return fire. Nigel spun round, 'Mum, this is *so sick*. What the fuck kind of a set-up is this?'

'Hey, look whatever...' Johnson began

Nigel leaped forward- 'Shut the fuck up. You've said enough. And you' -pointing to the two in the van- 'did you know about this?'

'Well, not really, but I wondered,' said Trevor

'You wondered! What a fucking scientist!'

Stella tried to get closer to her boy, her face creased in guilt and sorrow, but he pushed her away. Wiz threw his arm round Nigel's shoulder.

'Nige. Think about the Stones. Think about the mad poets. They all lived their lives as they felt. Your mum's a *big girl*. Look - we'll drop everyone off and I'm gonna take you to the shebeen.'

'Fuck that.'

Nigel leant his head on his arms against the whitepaint wall top as Wiz unlocked the bass flightcase and Stella's floppy overnight bag from the back of the van. He climbed back in with a doorslam, not looking back at the odd couple as they climbed the steps to the front door. Wiz got back in too, and they were away again. As Nigel, Sam and Trevor had lost their habitual after-gig verbosity, none of them feeling able to spark off a conversation again, he stuck on a tape- Axiom Funk - loud.

Not by accident, Nigel was the last in the van, and Wiz made him help unload the gear to store.

'Now my boy,' as he locked up the garage, 'it's time for a drink. Whadda you say?'

'What? At this time? It's…'

'Yeah! After twelve. But I know somewhere here. It's handy.'

They walked to a nearby row of shops; dark - but for a dim light in the glass above one featureless door. Wiz pressing the buzzer three times. Waited. The door opened by a five-foot-nothing lady of thirty; they followed her along the corridor to a door leading to stairs down to a basement bar. Several dark-skinned gentleman drinkers round a small pool-table greeting Wiz in a language Nigel didn't recognise but heard as musical.

At ten in the morning Stella was relaxing in the bath when Johnson grinningly jogged into the bathroom, raising his knees high as he came. He half-jumped into the bath, splashing wet all over the floor.

'Oooh Mr Johnson! What will the neighbours think!'

It was an average little bath with barely enough room for one, and although it was pleasant enough to share for a few minutes, they agreed to get out and get civilised again. But they kneeled down on the wet floor, pressed against each other. Their skin slippery, they fell gently to the hard wet lino and made love again. They rolled and ground slowly against the curled edges of the lino tiles which cut into them, leaving long scratches. Blood oozed from their skins and left little trails on the floor.

Stella insisted on buying a 'proper' breakfast at the local Italian café. 'That bath wasn't much good - I could be doing with another one now.'

'You got a shower at home though - that's better.'

'Yes... Tell you what. I don't have a day job, and neither have you. Come and see Chiswick.'

'Chiswick? Your home? Won't Oscar...'

'He's away. Come and have a look. You can play with the shower, and I'll show you the Eyot.'

'Eyot?'

'Island. It's old English, I think. Doesn't matter. It's a nice place - for a visit.' sighing, 'But I miss town. Anyway…'

'All right! I'll come. Whatever!'

A tube ride from East Putney to Stamford Brook and they had a ten-minute walk to their destination. After a quick guided tour of the house - skipping the door in the entrance hall - 'That was Trevor's room. For a whole year. It's just a store now,' said Stella - everything, to Johnson's eyes, looked like white on white: from the white walls to the cream bedroom carpet to the big white bed, sun broadcast through the white gauze curtains - they stripped off and shared the shower, which adjoined the bedroom, Stella had turned on the radio to the jazz station, although they couldn't hear much under the water. They scrubbed each other's backs and rubbed each other's fronts.

'What?' she asked- 'What? I didn't say-'

'That voice! My name!'

'Stella.'

She turned away from the shower to the source of the voice. A dark figure. Oscar.

'Ohmygod. Oscar.'

Johnson spun round too. Oscar had gone again. Stella turned off the water.

It must have been about ten am, judging by the traffic noise. Henry turned over, opened one eye and focused on his watch. Good guess. Close. He didn't feel as rough as he should have; but he had a raging thirst. He felt his way round the little kitchen for the 'clean' glass, filled it and drank so fast it hurt. Felt like a knot in the gullet. Then he sat on the bed for a moment, head resting on his hands. He would have to face handing back those keys to that creep. Why on earth did he let him talk him into staying here? He could have got back to 'home' easily enough.

The keys were on the table: a Yale and a mortice. He took them, let himself out, locked the door and made for downstairs. Room five. Rang the bell - thirty seconds and the girl, said in a deep voice, 'Helllo...' as she opened the door and looked up from under her eyelashes. Stood there, appraising the stranger as if the first time. A voice from the back: 'Let him in, baby - I *know* who that'll be.'

She stood back with a mocking welcome gesture - as Henry entered he noticed her red high heels. Number five was unexpectedly luxurious: it smelled of apple-rose and the darkly painted room was dominated by a giant TV screen and stereo system. Richard, in black, half-reclining on a black sofa.

A younger man - a kid, really, in a tight suit was parked on another chair in the corner, hands tapping a rhythm on his thighs and well into a triumphant boast,. 'all I did was look at 'im, just like that, and you shoulda seen 'im run! He'-

The kid caught Henry's eye and shut up.

'Yeah, nice one.' said Richard; he turned to Henry: 'So - Good morning, my friend. Sleep well?'

'Yes, I think I...'

'The keys, please.'

'Of course. Here they are.' -handing them over as the girl watched

'You thinking of staying, I hope?'

'Oh, no. I really would have got the Tube last night if I...'

'Heyy That's really too bad. I could have given you a real good deal. And you got the first night free.'

'Well it was very kind of you. I appreciate it.'

'I'm glad to help people whenever I can. In this life... Hey, look - I did something for you. And you can do me a favour, in return.'

Henry had turned to leave but noticed that the girl had shut the door. Richard was standing now, moving forward.

'I've got this friend - A friend of mine is driving over to your... side of town - you can get a lift with him - just help him make a delivery, okay?'

'What, right now?'

'Yes, you wanna get home dontcha. You're on my time now. Sit down. Get comfortable.'

It was an order. He sat in the dusky pink armchair while the girl fetched a white instant coffee-'Sugar?' 'Two, please'- and Richard spoke quietly to his phone. Only time for a few sips of coffee before he was ushered out to the street. As they left the entrance a matt-finish blue Ford Fiesta drew up. Richard spoke to the driver, a man of twentyfive in a shabby suit, and opened the back door for Henry to join the passenger, who wore a tie but with a grubby sports bomber jacket. A convivial slap on the back from Richard as Henry got in and pulled the door shut. Foot hard down on the floor - they skidded away; Henry aware that his host had been anything but genial, silently rejoicing over what he felt was an escape. His fellow travellers not speaking yet - but they were heading west.

Oscar striding back and forth in the kitchen, like a caged animal. Wet-haired Stella wrapped in her clothes entered, sat down at the farmhouse table on the other side from him. The kitchen smaller than usual, lit by the dull afternoon sun.

'You weren't coming back till tomorrow...'

'So! Would it have made any difference? You in the shower with a fucking Arab?'

'He's not an Arab. He's…'
'I don't give two fucks what he fucking is.'
picking up the microwave. Yanked it from the
wall socket, smashed it on the tiles. 'I'm not up
for this. I don't need this kind of crap.'
Stella's chair scraped backwards
'And you're some kind of angel? Don't think I
don't know about you and those *office girls*. You
were so obvious - I could tell just by your
smirk.'
'Oh, now you want to play clever do you?'
'Yes and I'll bet you weren't alone in Paris…'
'That's different! I was away!'
'What! I don't *believe* this. You're such a fucking
spoiled brat and you expect me to join the other
idiots. Don't come near me.'
Oscar going round the table; Stella jumping to
her feet and backing towards the door, Johnson
appeared and put a protective arm round her
'Johnny - please let's just get out of here for
now.'
'That's right. Don't come fucking back.' -
following them as they rushed through the
hallway to the front door

She did return, some days later, with Wiz and his van, to remove everything she valued before they brought in estate agents. And she didn't feel entirely happy about leaving any of her possessions alone in the house with Oscar. First they delivered her clothes and music to Johnson's flat. She had already moved in by increments - part of him felt that he really aught to resent the gradual intrusion, but he told himself she was exotic, and that her connections with the jazz scene and by extension, The Sixties, held his attention. He thought about her half-memories of Soho, their being together and her stage persona. It might spark his creativity: a world from where he could draw songs; but he imagined that he would slowly grow more interested in using her little history and her style, as he saw it, to promote her as a performer.

After the stop at Johnson's, most of the rest went to Wiz's garage beside the bulk of The Slakers' gear and the leatherette back seat out of the van. She sat as he backed up to the entrance; one of a line of lock-ups; jumped out and unlocked the padlock and mortice, lifting the flaky blue up-and-over door. 'Well, this is it. You always travel light?'

'Really, all I had that mattered was my piano. The books are mostly Oscar's, really.'

'A pi-a-no?'

'Wurlitzer. It was badly fucked. Not just the tines. Cheaper to sell it and... get a new one. But I never got round to getting the new one.'

'Don't mind dear. I can get one, easy. They're cheaper every day. Keyboards, all sorts.'

'Could you? I'd like a keyboard of some kind. Just to play with. Maybe write.' She knew about his borstal days and later, the time he did for 'a little petty theft' - it had left him with a weary but philosophical acceptance of life as it comes; he was always effortlessly considerate, but she did not want to know any details about getting keyboards. She was round the side of the van and looking to see what to lift first as Wiz had already begun carrying boxes into the back of the garage. She hardly knew where to start. 'You want this over. I can see that,' he said, ' why not just sit down, take it easy and I'll do the loading.' Wiz looked at her. She sighed, smiling sadly. Picked at the elbow hole in Wiz's jumper. He looked down. He put his other arm gently round her shoulders. 'Eh...'

They drew close, pressed tightly together. Their noses touched - she could smell diesel on his face. He pressed his face into her hair.

Something clicked: in her it was desperation to lose herself; in his trousers a familiar and willing response leapt. They edged carefully round the stored band gear and machine parts to the seating. As they lay down on the leatherette there was a loud creaking of springs. It was dark in the back of the garage. They squirmed sluggishly on the bench, the steel supports scraping in a slow rhythm on the concrete floor. Her medium-short skirt rode up. She pulled his hand away from her breast, bit-scraped his fingers, while pulling down her panties just enough for his long slow entry. His hand left her mouth and dug into her hair before hooking over the seat back. They nearly fell to the floor as they began approaching orgasm, but she gripped his hips, pulling him into her and he steadied them with his other hand below on the crumbly concrete. She managed not to cry out - they were oblivious to the small dog that wandered into the room out of the sun, tentatively lifted his leg twice and then left, having decided not to bother leaving a mark.

The car slowed as they neared Edgware Road. Maybe he could just leave here... The front passenger turned, said, 'Okay. We're going to visit a customer. Do a collection. You just come up too okay?'

'Wha-' he raised his arm over the seat back, waved it to silence Henry, 'Just follow us, right.'

The car turned off through the street market and they stopped at the entrance to a brickbuilt block of flats. The two men got out, the driver motioning Henry to join them as he locked up. They entered the block, climbed the stairs to the third landing; the driver rang a doorbell and simultaneously began kicking the door. As he did, the passenger handed Henry a brown paper bag containing something heavy and hard. The door opposite opened, the tousled face of Jerry Parkin looked out, blanched and withdrew.

Kicked the door again. It flew open. A big man, iron bar in hand. He was unshaven, wearing a dirty vest, shapeless trousers. Henry's two acquaintances fell back - they hadn't expected this. But the passenger received a blow to the head resulting in heavy flow of blood. A bang. Henry's ears imploded in the narrowness of the landing. The big man's chest exploded red, his vest wet red, he fell back against the doorway. The driver spun round, grabbed Henry by the shoulder. Thrust another heavy paper bag inside Henry's jacket and grabbed bag number one. The two hoods turned and pitter-pattered down the stairwell; Henry half-ran half-fell as he followed. At street level the car screeched away as he reached the pavement - stumbling off in the other direction. A little boy and a little girl watched, she made a loud hiccupping noise; both giggled at the stumbling man.

He 'knew' but could not believe what was in his paper bag. He circled back round to Edgware Road, crossed and walked slowly down behind the police station, along Church Street to the old graveyard, where he found a seat. He peeled open the bag. Laughed quietly, but the laughter was choked by a gulp. It wouldn't fit in his pocket, but he found that if he took it out of the bag, it would just go into his inside breast pocket, already badly stretched by carrying that mobile phone. Which, as was his habit, remained at what he still though of as home. He rolled the bag into a ball and jammed it between the bench planks, took a deep breath. His diaphram convulsed once, twice - gorge rose - but nothing came up. It was nearly eleven and he hadn't eaten. He wasn't sure if he wanted to eat.

Stella hid away for one week in a bed-&-breakfast, the day after she had gone back to Johnson's, without telling him her plan. The B&B was in a quiet side street, identical to the other brick houses in the terrace except for its front garden containing an ancient motorbike sidecar. She had no plan, so this was easy; but sharing a room with a stranger, a woman from Birmingham who spoke in embittered tones about her ex-husband, the DSS, everything in sentences that came out as chopped-off soundbites was wearing. Although the roundabout in the middle of Hammersmith was a building site, its shops and the pub round the back gone, she found a café in the road way beyond the Cinema; somewhere ordinary where she could sit for afternoons and just watch the passing scene outside. From her new base she was able to get back to wander her old home-ground, Soho. She had kept her Union membership, 'just in case', so she was able to join Ronnie Scott's Club for thirty pounds - she had never got round to joining when she was working, so it felt like making an important connection. Just to show willingness to The Establishment, she visited the Job Centre twice. Friday night, she got to the Club early, in time for a front-row seat in the slightly non-smoking area, using her 3p ticket voucher for the first of several red wines. She didn't pay a lot of attention to the support band: watching them do their thing but somehow not hearing anything, as she worried at the changes of the past week. She enjoyed Ronnie's address to the audience, by now approaching capacity, and laughed in the right places; especially when he said, 'These are The Jokes.' Marion Montgomery, the star attraction, had the audience singing one line while she danced over it - Stella added a harmony and was rewarded with a raised sisterly eyebrow. After the next song, Marion adding mysterious and sinuously sinister undertones to 'The People That You Never Get To Love', Stella had to leave. No question of waiting for the second set. She could no longer take it in for thinking about her own desires. Her mind was racing.

She was in trouble, too. She managed to catch the late train back but without her own key, she had to ring the doorbell at 1.30. The little Armenian lady of the house opened the door as far as the chain would allow, half whispering - 'What you want? You are very late my dear.'

'Oh, I really am sorry - I hadn't realised it was so late.'

'Well I let you in. I am upset.'

She also had to insinuate herself back into her shared room, taking the greatest care to avoid the creaky floorboard; but in the dark banging her knee on her neighbour's bed. She lay there, staring at the ceiling in the blackness, for hours, regretting having come back instead of seeing the whole gig. Thinking about singing. About what she should have been doing for ages instead of retiring to bloody Chiswick. It was OK in the summer. Just that first summer...

'Where the fuck did you go, Stella? I thought you went back to the house.'

'Oh, baby, just let me lie down for a bit!' - sitting down on the tarred top step outside Johnson's front door, she bowed her head, cradled her knees, and sobbed quietly. He wasn't sure at first what to do, but put his hand, awkwardly, in her hair then sat beside her, his arm folding round her back. Her hair smelt of tobacco smoke and something expensively sharp and musky. After a few minutes they went inside, up to his flat.

'You not married?' he asked one afternoon, 'No - he wanted to, crazy guy. But it was just too far for me. Well, if we had, I could have stung him for something. But he saw us.' - 'So who gets what, then?' - 'I'm back where I was, but older. The house - he got the mortgage, but he never got to paying it off. It's all empty shit, honey.'

'So, like, is 'e Nige's old man?'

'Well, no, that was, Someone else.'

'Oh, I see. So that's why he hates the fucker so much.'

'Does he, really? Oh, yes, I know he did. They hated each other. Oscar started the hating though. He treated Nige like a rival!'

'I bet Nigel felt the same way too'

'Same way? Well... Okay - he slept in my bed when he was a baby,'

She got up, walked through to the little kitchen, ran cold tap water into a glass. Gulped. Sighed; looked round towards the window. 'Well, you may as well know. It was his brother.'

'His brother?'

'Yeah. Not part of my scene, but we met because he drank at some of the gigs I did. He drank a lot. He didn't want to know when I got pregnant. He was just bloody immature.' She leant her elbows on the counter below the window, held her face in her hands. 'So who needs him. Either of them. Fuck.' She was crying silently. Johnson came to her, put his arms round her, breathing into her hair.

He was becoming more aware of how dependent Stella was on him. She could be, as the barriers of politeness broke down, as manipulative as she was generous. She found out his favourite Fender bass strings and bought him a set, plus two sets of Rotosound on the side. If they went to the cinema and she paid, she liked to give him the tickets to hold, as it was his task as her personal Alpha Male. But she found ways of tricking him out of going places by himself sometimes, or into taking her along. He could easily forget how vulnerable she felt - she had given up more than he had for their time together, although not at all unwillingly; but she was conscious of having made mistakes in her life and needed to turn it round before it was too late.

He was beginning to feel that his flat in south London was getting too tiny for both of them to inhabit full time. Despite that, when she suggested finding somewhere bigger his first feeling was of being pulled away from his chosen place in life.

Then, as he began feeling regret at having lost his 'single' status, he remembered his original thoughts about making this his career, and turning it into a business. Although he kept his ideas about management to himself, they were able to talk things through - writing songs together made it mandatory to keep an openness.

She was so unlike his mother, a bit floppy in places, he thought, but almost skinny like him when Mum was small and round and...motherly. He was attracted to the hard lines of her face as much as she was taken by his youthful solicitude. He loved the way her lips became sluttishly swollen as she rode him, hair hanging down to her breasts. She impaled, looking down on his glistening eyes, buried in his dark, softly determined face.

Stella, living on Social Security now like her young lover, was enjoying a rerun of her not-so-distant darkly groovy adolescence as they aspired to greatness together. A good deal of her leaning on Johnson sprung from needing him as an audience to watch her act the part of a naïve pop hopeful, as she couldn't easily revisit the routine by herself without scepticism.

The assiduous Wiz indulged her by taking Johnson for late-night drinking sessions at one or another of his favourite shebeens; and benevolently took off some of the pressure in the love affair by inviting Stella back to his bed-sit on occasional afternoons; invitations that reassured her, and which she was glad to accept. It was refreshing to be able to get dirty with someone who was, in fact, a little older, and who didn't need to have old things, old stories, explained. He was also without beer belly - his bony white frame a contrast to Johnson's adolescent softness - a good slow fuck, and he could be trusted to keep it to himself.

Henry was watching his brother introduce a mono-browed punky-looking girl on the TV, and she was waving something that looked like a snake made from glue. He couldn't raise enough interest to get off the sofa and turn up the volume. He was drunk. He had been down at the studio since five-thirty, and spent an entire evening ruining several attempts at making serious sculpture. He had wished he had some of that dope now, but made do with a pub crawl back from the Bush, starting from the end of the Market and weaving back through Latimer Road. He gradually blacked out.

At four in the morning he opened his mind to a blank blue screen and pisswet trousers.

The next afternoon, having toyed with adding his pub-crawl wetsuit to the day's washing, he put his trousers in a plastic bag and binned them; but did his laundrette run anyway. While he was watching the drier tumbling he could see Jerry Parkin across Powis Terrace with a chap in a suit; seemed to be pointing, under duress, to the shop.

At night, he ate a takeaway from round the corner and sat down to look at The Gun. Although it looked smaller than at first, and neat, it was heavy - they didn't look this heavy in the films. He wondered if he could use it. He pointed it at the bookshelf and gently pulled the trigger. He was sweating. Nothing happened. Christ! What a relief. The safety catch. There it is. Now, what happens, if

Jesus fucking Christ I've shot the ceiling

The doorbell rang; he ignored it. Rang again. He decided to apologise to the neighbours about the noise, walked to the door, turned the knob and it flew open as the Two Hoods ran in. He recognised the first as the driver, although there was a deep cut over one eye.

'We came for that gun. You took it.'

'We-ell, you gave it to me, remember.' -his heart beat shot up as he fell back against the wall

'Give us the gun.'

'How did you find me?'

The Second Hood added, 'Just hand us the fuckin gun, right?'

The driver pushed past Henry and both intruders strode into the kitchen. Henry followed, leaving the door open.

'Now what the fuck? I didn't ask you in.'

'You weren't meant to keep the gun.'

'Why did you fucking give it to me then?'

'What?'

'The gun.'

'We're taking it back.'

'What makes you think I want to fucking keep it?'

'Just hand it over,' said Hood Two, standing back.

'Nice and quiet.'

'This is my house-'

'And we'll be on our way, quiet like.'

'And I didn't ask you in.'

'We don't want to waste anyone's time.'

'Well, you're wasting mine.'

Henry ceased caring much about anything; least of all the demands being made by his guests.

'Here it is.', - he strode into the back room and picked up the little machine from the couch, pointed at them, his face, below a dusting of ceiling white, a mask of grimness. Their attitude changed radically - the driver turned away, put his hand on the other's arm; they both bowed a little and began walking backwards to the door, let themselves out and vanished. He hadn't thought it might be that easy. He couldn't stop himself giggling after a minute. Then he laughed again. He felt exhilarated but uneasy. His heart was pounding.

He sat down at the table.

Rested his chin on his hands.

Closed his eyes.

Opening them again, he looked slowly round the room, holding his breath.

Thought: A pact between me and these four walls. The gluey silence joins us. If I step outside and get knocked down and killed I won't ever experience these walls again.

It won't matter to me.

He still held the gun. He breathed in deeply; this brought on a fit of coughing as he inhaled dry, sooty plaster from his sleeve.

After half an hour he decided to risk going out; he hid the gun inside the couch, with its heavy finish of dirtywhite powder, between the springs and looked out both ways, locked up carefully and headed towards Wormwood Scrubs.

He took a deliberately tortuous route to North Pole Road and crossed the freeway of Scrubs Lane, clambering over to the greenery.

Standing in the middle of Wormwood Scrubs. It was almost quiet, above the thin warm blanket of distant London roar. Some ambient light bled over his head towards the trees. He suddenly realised in the rare moment of calm, his mind totally relaxed, a complete lack of self-consciousness:

This is what 'it' is: the pact between the trees and me.

Not me.

Not the trees.

It's the go-between that is existence.

I pick it up at my end - so *existence* exists.

CLIFF G HANLEY

Six

The old car had been parked two streets away, for over a month; Henry had meant to try selling it - he could have used the money - but kept 'forgetting' to get it organised. It was no more than a damp store on wheels for stuff he hadn't bothered to throw away, and in such an advanced state of degeneration that no one had attempted a break-in. Although it was almost summer and quite warm, it did take some revving-up to get started, though. He had decided to take Richard's gun back. He couldn't relax with the thing in the house. An artist with no job, a dead wife, nothing to say, but within grasping distance of satori. With a gun.

There was a youth in a suit outside flat five - not one of The Hoods, but one who was obviously not willing to move aside. He looked at Henry with a mixture of fear and suspicion. The door opened, a man in a dark blue raincoat came out and seeing Henry, immediately looked away avoiding eye-contact; heading past to the stairwell door. An upward gust of piss-air as he passed through the door. The kid folded himself into Number Five and there were mumbled words exchanged. A clap of hands. Richard appeared, face bland, segueing into a mask of bonhomie

'Ah, my friend! Come in, come in. You did me a great favour, and I want you to know I'm very grateful.' arm round the shoulder - more than Henry had wanted. A quick drop-off of the offending article would have been enough. He allowed himself to be escorted into the tiny enclave. The girl wasn't here this time. They were alone.

'Look. I don't see why you wanted me to go to that place. I didn't have anything to do with what happened there.

'You were *there*. You were...Part of it.'

'It was nothing to do with me. I didn't want to be there in the first place.'

'Okay! Don't worry about it. Your secret's safe with me.'

'*My* secret? Look- Whatever fucking scam you're up to-' 'Hey, hey, relax. That's enough. Sit down...Henry.'

'I'd rather leave. I-'

'Siddown. And listen to what I say.'

'Why the fuck should I-'

Richard forced him down by the shoulder, into the armchair. Smiled grimly, You're in this now and you can make something out of it. If you get smart. Tell you what. How would you like to do some, like, casual work for me. It'll be well paid. Always pays well.'

'But I...'

'And you'll be able to get that Mercedes, holiday in Ibiza, whatever. You can just partner one of my boys on his round. No sweat. For a couple weeks.'

'Look, I can do without Ibiza. I just came to bring you -'

'Ah yes you got a little something we left with you. You're a good man. It's good we met. Came all this way. You took the trouble. Honest. I *respect* that... So where is it?'

Henry squirmed to one side and reached into his baggy inside pocket; Richard instinctively reared back a little but smiled as Henry brought out the gun and offered it up, handle first. As he handled scissors in the studio. Richard taking it, laying it with care on the floor behind the giant TV. Henry half-raised himself, turning towards the door but Richard gripped his arm, 'The boy'll be here real soon. In an hour or less. Watch the news.' - picking up a remote control as Henry sat, his head spinning slightly, hands sweating; two clicks to the bighaired lady on CNN. Richard explained that the work was just a matter of collecting rents and debts. Henry knew that it was liable to involve more unpleasantness.

'Look, don't forget I've already seen what this "collecting" business is about.'

'Ooh, don't worry man - that was strictly a one-time thing, goes well back. And I can well do without that kind of aggravation. But that boy was well out of order. Cost me big time to fix it too. What you can do will be… more laid back. Whadda ya say?'

(A) They knew where he lived. (B) He needed some purpose in life. (C) Why should he care, really?

He wiped the sweat from his forehead.

'Look. Whatever you're doing. I'm an artist, not a bleeding heavy.' - '…An artist, eh? Don't forget you were part of that…visit. That's just gonna be you and me, and that's cool, we're friends. It don't go out of this room. You can make good now, understand? It's just between us.'

Richard taking Henry by the shoulders and lifting him to his feet - 'Sure you do! Hey - can you paint my portrait?' -'Maybe...' ' -That's real cool. I couldn't draw a line to save my life. Art, that's special. Make money at it then?'

'Sometimes. Um.'

'Hey... You were in on that touch. Only you and I know. But I can keep schtum. Understand?'

Henry thinking about how he would have been interested if he could have used the experience for art; but now all he wanted was an escape from his non-life- 'I'll think about it, okay?' He turned to the door. Richard put his hand against the door, 'Take your time. It's a *good gig.*'

He dropped his hand. Henry pulled the door open, stepped out, and left, 'All right - I just might...' 'Yeah! That's cool man! Half an hour.'

He left the building, walked through the sunlit brick-lined streets to his parked car. He almost got in; after resting his arm for a moment on the sun-heated roof he turned back. Walked more slowly but slightly back-tracking by a different route. A pet shop. He gazed mindlessly into the fish tank. Out of the side of his eye he noticed Hood Number Two, loitering by the corner, watching him. He decided not to 'see' him.

At number five: 'Look...How about if I give it a shot. For a week, just.'

'A week! That's really cool. It'll be a *nice little earner* for you, too.' Richard welcomed Henry back into his flat and gave him the armchair again, but without force.

The 'boy', when he arrived, was Hood Number Two.

'Henry. This is Simon. He'll show you the ropes, keep an eye on you.' - gesturing 'stand up', he put his arm round Henry's shoulders and escorted them both out of the door - ' You can do the local ones today - won't take long. And my friend. Anything you need to know, just ask me later. Simon knows the score. Simple credit control. It's just a matter of doing good business. You can drive his car for now, okay?'

They visited three addresses and he only had to stand outside the car while Simon collected money or did some kind of deal at the door. He had a vague plan to leave now and forget about all of this, but the right moment didn't seem to come.

Simon, although he knew where he was going and what he had to do, gradually revealed himself as being a little out of his depth. Before they visited one flat near Peckham, he said, 'We decided to give this guy just one more week to pay up, and he didn't shift. So we have to, like, encourage him.'

Henry stood and watched as Simon rang the
bell. The door opened. A face. Door closed a
little; the face reappeared with a small paper
bag. Simon took it, grabbed the face by its nose,
gave a sharp twist. As he returned, Henry
suddenly felt quite ill. Not the first time he had
got into the wrong job by increments. They left
in the car, Henry on the wheel, leaning his arm
out of the opened window as Simon wiped the
blood on the paper bag.

'What the hell was that all about?'

Simon said nothing.

'Look - what you did there - what's going on?'
-Henry was almost shouting

'It's the word I got. Wot to do.' Simon looked
huffy, belligerent.

'Well maybe you could think twice about that.'
-Henry felt quite angry, more with himself for
taking this on, than with Simon for being a
thug; but Hood Number Two took it
personally. As they drove away he appeared to
shrink a little, and when courtesy of his
navigation they stopped in a back-street off
York Road, the visit was less traumatic: a mere
handing over of money, accepted.

Simon said, summoning up all his bravado, 'We
told most of these people to keep good time.
Most of them are okay. Somadem not so good.'

Henry hated being pressured into this 'work' - everything about it smelt bad, especially the dreadfully smarmy Richard, and he felt dishonest in having anything to do with it; but he told himself it was more 'interesting' than being dead. The worst part, though, was that it hadn't been his decision. He could have walked away, now. He didn't.

After the day was done, Henry tried handing in his notice. 'I've done some driving for you now. Look. This is not for me. I'm out of the game.'

'You gotta week ahead. You'll wanna come back, Friday. I'll have a wad of crisp ones for you.'

'I don't want them.'

'Yeah? How much do you not want 'em?'

Henry realising his 'mentor', although he was a good little thug, was no organiser and compensated by talking up his role in the decision process. 'We' rarely included Simon, if he was talking about decision-making. The more he did it, the more it was obvious that he was a lowly and inferior enforcer; and felt it. Henry, driving the old Ford and watching Simon go through his routine, gradually came out of his cocoon of alienation, as he realised how insecure the little hard man was, and gradually reassumed his lecturer persona as he learned more about the nature of the work. He began to suspect that he had been given a spurious reputation of some sort: he had expected to be ordered around by his companion, but Simon kept a nervous, almost defensive, front up when they talked. He seemed unwilling or unable to really push his opinion at Henry. The balance of power between them altered completely in a few weeks, with Henry gently suggesting modes of behaviour towards regular customers, timely payers and debtors. At first he felt it difficult persuading Simon to lay off the violence, but his confidence grew to the point where he felt able to say, 'Simon. This one's an old bloke. He's maybe just lost the plot. Just be *firm*.'

Simon stared out of the rainy windscreen, his jaw grinding, eyes narrowing.

'Okay.' - a short, willing-to-please tone

It was impossible to make any sense of the 'business'. Little by little it became clearer that it was split in two areas: nothing more than collecting rent money and either taking advance payments for supplying drugs or chasing up late arrears. The rent was from some double-address claimant scams. As for the occasional bit of heavy enforcement: he gradually became inured to it, as it concurrently shifted down to threats and a little bit of pushing. He was regressing to the relationship he had suffered with his bossy, younger brother since childhood, but found that he was able to reverse the roles with just a little firmness of voice, an ability nurtured in teacher training. He was beginning to enjoy this, as he was able to sell it to himself as exactly that - an extension of his career. After some weeks it was Henry who was reporting to Richard and setting up the agenda. The role that Hood Number One must have played. He was never able to find out what had become of him.

At first they only dealt in money; they never saw the drugs, but it had been mostly crack cocaine for three years. And the rents, in flats relatively guaranteed to be ignored by the Metropolitan Police, thanks to an arrangement of which he was as yet ignorant.

He could see that the DSS fraud line was more effort than it was really worth; the setting up of fake addresses, and the amassing of little sums by fiddling with multiple rent books. Richard kept it going to give him the semblance of authority. But the drug supplier, Henry was increasingly curious about. He learned that there was more than one. When they stopped at a terrace house near Wandsworth, he joined Simon at the door. After a rattle of the Victorian letterbox, the door opened slowly. The pallid face of a youth, about 20, unfashionably long, dirtyblond hair, stubbly chin. 'Hello... Mark,' said Simon, pushing the door farther.

'Oh. Oh, yes! Do come in, man. Got a new arrival yesterday. Straight from the -uh- source.' His polite voice and inquisitively-arched eyebrows reminded Henry of one or two students he had had in his groups, straight from 'public' school. He and Simon followed as Mark opened the door and turned back inside. A few scarves hanging on nails over an old mattress leaning against the wall; some clothes, a milk bottle on the bare floor. In a dimly-lit room off the hallway, Mark sat down on an old chair, reaching down behind the sofa parked in front of the partially curtained bay window. He brought out a half-pint sized plastic bag, full of rocky white powder.

'Where d'you get this, then?' -'The usual place, man. It's kosher.' -he gave a little guffaw- 'Like, it's from the vaults, man! It's weighed, okay. You'll see the bag's still sealed, too. Seven fifty okay?'

'You were told four, weren't you.'

'Heyy, man, loosen up-'

'Three I got here, look. (counting rapidly, like a cardsharp) And two more for the supply. Take it and keep your nose clean. You get kickbacks anyway.'

'Aw, shit, I say-' Simon took the bag and shoved Mark hard enough to land him sprawling on the sofa.

'You need us to deal this out and you need to keep your end up. That's all. Here's the money.' Thrusting a bunch of paper. - 'Fuck you, you're keeping it for yourself. This isn't half of what-' Mark blocking Simon's exit. Simon's knee up to the groin; as Mark jerked forwards Simon pushed him to the side on the floor. Two heavy kicks to the head. Throwing down the money as he turned and pushed Henry towards the door. Henry stopped him outside. 'Hey, don't stop here, we gotta go on. Can't stay here.'

'Simon. I'm not fucking interested in playing your fucking little gangster games. Behave your fucking self.'

'Yeh, but let's move, come on. Go.'

'Remember what I said. You can get people on your side. You don't have to keep pushing them.'

Simon, looking down and nodding vigorously, behaved as if he was listening to what he was being told, but he was more concerned with getting away. He didn't like getting this close to the top end. Putting pressure on cunts was better. He found the new guy difficult to understand. He was supposed to be clued-up, but he kept asking questions. And if Simon put on a show of strength for him, he objected. And Richard says don't knock him about; we need him!

Unaware of this confusion, Henry realised anyway that he would have to take the lead role from now on, whenever possible.

'Right, this next one's just to pay rent for two places.' said Henry as they got back in the car, 'Where did that stuff come from, then? -'Like he said, from the source.' -'So he's just a middleman...' -'Middleman that's right' -'What happens to that stuff?' -'Oh, it comes back. Cooked. It's sorted, gets passed on.' -'What, do you mean he weighs it, then?' -'Yeah, that's right...'

Simon was behind the wheel; they pulled away
'You don't sound so sure.'
'Whatever.'

One day, as he was walking to the Tube station for another day of 'collections' he thought about his blue suede shoes, quietly speaking, 'You look like a *pansy* moi san.'

An old lady across the street looked up at him. She couldn't have heard his fake east-end voice over the morning babble of the Portobello Road stalls.

The bank on the corner. One time he used the cash machine he had remembered: Angela was always complaining that he didn't 'connect' with her - he dismissed such new-age hippy babble. Then she killed herself. Some fucking driver. One speed.

He turned into the cheap shoeshop for a pair of stout brogues, change out of a fiver. Nearly took the suedes back home but left them in the street bin. Took them out again, left them in Oxfam's doorway. And so the good hustler went to work, passing the Sally Army, the fake-old-map table and turning out of the Road at the fish stall.

Oscar and his three fellow conspirators found themselves setting up in business before they had planned: getting the licence had taken a few years and it had been difficult keeping their plans low-profile. So many others had taken the low-risk option of setting up independent production companies to carry on doing more or less what they had been doing before, but starting a TV company was another game entirely, and involved backers. Their accountant gradually took on the role of Programme Scheduler, and they shopped around for a new firm, while taking on someone to bring in advertisers. At the same time, two of the gang including Oscar were finding their contracts being wound down. In his case it was due to an external policy review identifying shrinking audiences for arts programmes. They began working up to a schedule of test transmissions during the 'dead' daytime spots.

Henry's life now routinely involved regular days 'at work' in his new straight job in business. When he didn't feel uneasy, he felt motivated. After he had turned up at Number Five expecting another day of quiet credit control, to find the boss was out, or when there was a change in the routine, he began spending more time in the flat upstairs. One day when there was no rain, he dismantled the ancient bed and took it in pieces down to the bins, then walked around the local streets, finding a second-hand furniture shop with a decent bed. It looked good enough through the window, but he had to enter the shop and try sitting on it. No creaks. 'Yes, it's in good nick. Good as new. You can have it today for, well, eighty-five quid. Cutting my own throat.'

'Can you do a delivery?'

'Oh, I dunno about today. Have to speak to my bruvvah. Give me five minutes, I'll call him.'

He disappeared to the back of the shop. After a while, shouted, 'Can do my son! He'll be here in a couple hours.'

While he waited in the pub, he toyed with the idea of a 'salesman with his throat cut' sculpture. Could he do it in clay? Or just make it out of wood? But really - was it worth it: going back to being an artist so that he could recycle an old surrealist idea? No - better leave it out.

From the air of relaxed anarchy and especially the constant smell of dope smoke almost outweighing the cabbage-piss reek ingrained in the bricks, Henry had picked up the impression that the top floors in the tenement were somehow 'out of bounds' to the police - although it was so quiet he couldn't imagine why it was so important that it should be some kind of fortress. One night, he had dosed off early on his new bed with a book. He woke to a party, taking in every flat and the corridor. A sound system at one end of the passage blasting sub-sonic bumps with earsplitting cymbals and synth at the other extreme, so loud that it felt to be coming from inside his mattress. He looked out and found himself in a solid crowd of ravers, the air thick with ganja. Shoes on, locked up, sidled out to High Street for a taxi back to Ladbroke Grove. He was only forking out thirty quid a week out of his earnings and felt he could painlessly treat the flat as a 'business expense'.

One day he told Richard that he had been looking at the relative income from various sources, and suggested he concentrate on property and class B drugs, as there was much less lost through bribery, or 'pay-off'.

'Hey, my man - you've been working well here. 'he looked quizzically at Henry- 'Have you been looking at the book?'

'Oh, no. Just guessing, from the kind of people we've been dealing with, the notes you gave me, the numbers...' -'Well, keep it that way. You're a quiet worker. You don't make trouble when there ain't no need for it. It's fine. Just leave the business end of it to me, will you?'

'Well - O.K. - But I'd think about it.' - he was about to leave - 'Just a, one more thing. That blond kid off York Road.' 'Yeh, what of im? Is he?'- 'He's just the middleman, who-' 'He shouldn't have been in on it, should never have been in, fuck' 'Then who-' 'Look - stick to your job and don't fuck with me okay?' Richard almost shouting. Henry backed off. He decided for once not to stay in the flat upstairs. He had made it clean enough to be habitable, accidentally discovering how to get the water heater going while poking about with a pencil; but something in Richard's manner suggested that it might be best to keep to his own side of town. His 'home' may have been scrubbed clean of his own smell, while holding too many regretful memories, but it was an extension of himself. As were the streets. He picked up a copy of Galleries Guide from one of the local galleries for the first time in almost a year, and decided, just to keep in touch with his 'old self', to do the West End openings the following week.

At the first gallery, hung with gloss-painted sheets of steel, he grabbed a glass of white (diet) and looked around for old faces. It was filling up quickly although it was only just after six. Mostly sharp-suiters, their backs to the wall, networking.

'-well most of the animals of course are all dead-'

'-it's a multi-faceted platform approach. '

't's a weekly arts thing-'

'-benches.' 'Bench paintings?' 'No just benches.'

'-said they'd freeze his assets-'

'rling you *look* rich-'

'-incrementally-'

'-nly another start-up company, I kid you not-'

'I'd stick with futures-'

'-mixed it with blood. Had to keep 'em outside-'

He recognised the gallery owner talking sales, tall and blonde, towards the back of the gathering crowd. Decided not to try waving to her; drank up. Back towards the street.

The next gallery was quieter, less jammed with business people. There was a small heap of anoraks on the floor inside, below the window. A tall, young, incredibly beautiful, mini-skirted dark-haired girl welcomed him at the door. 'Would you like a list?' -'Thanks.' -'The drinks are over there, on the table.'-she gave him a sheet of A4 paper and he made his way to the drinks table. Another wine. Red this time. He gulped, and looked at the wall opposite. The paintings were the kind of stuff he usually enjoyed: full of texture, earthy colour. No frames of course, á la mode. But somehow he couldn't bring himself to feel any of the old enthusiasm. Perhaps he was just getting jaded. Or had his taste changed?

'Henry, old boy. How have you been?' - Frank Martin, a regular face Henry knew just from nights like these and the occasional party, taller than him, and much more animated

'Frank. Good to see you again. I've been... doing lots of thinking about work.'

'Haha! That's the boy! Keep it going. Any shows coming up then?'

'No, not this year. Maybe next... it depends on what I can assemble. I could do with getting a new collection together.'

'Well, never say die. Tried the RA again this year, but got the usual knock back. Their loss! You got a drink?' -'Yes, I...' -'Oh of course, I didn't see it. Been round this one?' -'No, not yet.'

Well, wait till you hear what this boy's been up to!'

Frank leant forward, jabbing his finger in the face of his companion, who gently twisted his face away, one eye half-closed.

'Mirovich, how have you been?'

Mirovich, wilting slightly with Frank's arm heavily around his shoulder, was a one-man oasis of calm in the babble. He raised one hand a little in a polite gesture.

'So did you get into the Summer Show?' asked Henry

'No. But it doesn't matter. I'm having my own show at Number One London'

'Number One? Where the fuck is that?'

'It's only Wellington's house,' put in Frank with a big smile.

'Christ! Are you having to pay?'

Mirovich spoke so quietly that it was an effort for Henry to hear him. Despite himself he had to cross over the line into "interest".

'Pay? No. I never pay,' replied Mirovich.

-'Well, see you in a minute!' yelped Frank, as he Pulled Mirovich back into the crowd. Henry was about to follow them; Mr Punch and Robert Peel were circulating in there already. Always available for public appearances, together they had taken method acting to its extreme, and become their characters; Peel even changing his name by deed poll. Mr Punch wheeled out and grabbed henry's elbow. 'Henery! Stout fellow! Have you heard this one? What's the difference between an elephant and a bottle of wine?' -'...Dunno.' -'One of them is both the same! Haha!'

'You're getting better. Haven't I heard that...' 'Of course! The old ones are the best.' Henry ducked to one side as Mr Punch looked about to launch into a limerick, and gulped his wine. He felt unable to do the chummy act, not that it would have taken any effort; but it suddenly felt like an endurance test. He looked more at his fellow guests than at the pictures. Many of them were looking at the art on the walls; mostly couples - a group of, maybe, office girls, or students. They were connected to each other, to the rest of the crowd and to the stuff on the walls. As they swung past his eyes others took their place, like escaping fairground horses. Who *were* these people? And should he really care? They were living in a 'world' of brightly coloured inconsequence. He felt, creeping up the back of his neck an almost palpable sense of disconnection. He wasn't part of this!

One month later, Richard handed him, after his completion of the day's visits, a battered hard-cover notebook. 'Tell you what, now you've had a good look at how we do business, I want you t'check out these accounts. Take them home, will you. And here's your cut from today, in fives.' - pressing the book on Henry as he ushered him out of the door.

'I'm no accountant. I know fuckall about the way you've been working. How the hell can I...' Richard grabbed his shoulder. 'Here. Take this upstairs. You can keep it safe there.' 'Safe? What's wrong with...' 'Hey, my man, just stow it, ok?'

After he got in to his bachelor pad there were two loud bangs on the door, which opened. Richard again. 'Better stick this bag somewhere, too.' 'What's in...' 'Never mind,' hissed Richard, 'Just stuff I don't wanna keep down below for a couple days. Right?'

Henry looked at him for a moment. He was no longer the big-suited hustler. Hardly big enough to fill his black satin cowboy shirt, which hung crumpled and stained from his narrowing shoulders. 'Look. I've been doing your dirty work all day. I never asked you for this fucking job. I don't want to be looking after your business too. You can look after your fucking self.'

'Please. Just keep this bag. Stick it in the hole behind the cupboard. It'll only be for a couple days.'

'Well... all right. I don't want to know anything about it. Two days.'

'Two days. That's the least you can do! Look- you were with Simon when he knocked the boy around. Why didn't you stop him?'

'The boy? Whadda you mean? What boy?' - 'He was our front for the crack. Didn't you get that?'

'Look- you never let me in on any of-' 'You should've understood that. It was fucking plain. Now it's badly fucked up. Now, just stow this for a while. Okay?'

'All right. I'll stick it away. Don't *whine* at me, if you keep your bloody secrets.'

All the nasty feelings he had managed to paint over were breaking through; the soldier ants beetling out of the canvas. He put the bag, a used padded A3 mailbag, containing a few weighty objects, in the hole behind the kitchen cupboard, locked up and left with the 'accounts' book.

The girl was outside, two streets away. He immediately looked for her red shoes; but she was wearing dirty trainers with her denim jeans. She saw him looking. 'Yes you remember me. So you'll know me next time.'

'Are you going up?'

'Up there? To that bastard? No way.'

'Oh. I thought you were together-' 'He wanted me around, sure. But I got my own life, and he's got no respect.'

'He talks about it lots-' 'Talk! Look-' she turned up her face to the sky and he could see the bruising on her cheek, purple on dark brown skin - 'Fuck. He knocked you about?' 'Yes, he knocked me about. So fuck him.'

She was about to turn and stride away but Henry had to know more. 'You probably think this is a stupid question, but - did you tell the police?' 'The police?' her voice went up-register as her half-laughter was choked by her anger- 'He's *working* for the pigs.' He nearly followed her, before a rare, compressed largo of revelation as he examined her departing arse enabled him to understand that the urge to follow was nothing to do with solving any mystery and everything to do with sex. And that he would be wasting his time.

Johnson hadn't been altogether happy about going out to buy new bed sheets together. It felt like Real Commitment, when he had been able to persuade the late-starting rock rebel in him that this was only really an affair. Contrarily though, when Stella managed to get on the waiting list for a decent-sized housing trust flat, he felt better. It was more solid. He liked things organised and planned.

'Stella, I've got a session lined up for you.'

'For me? What about the band?'

'Well, okay, it's really a session. Doing some backing tracks in that studio in Basing Street.'

'Hah! All right honey. I'm not proud. How did you dig this up?'

'It was after that gig at the workingmen's club.' -'Yes, wasn't that funny. No cloth hats.' -'And I did a bit of phoning. It just could lead to something better. I know these guys have gotta hear you live.'

'Look. What about the band?'

'The band?

'Yes, the band.'

'It's doing okay. 'Okay, hell. You've been doing gigs but you don't hardly go to rehearse. And we haven't had a Chalice gig for a couple of weeks-' 'That's cool, really. Don't you think you could work up to a solo deal?'

'Solo deal? With who, for fuck's sake? Look, I just wanted to play with my boy, and' -'and he didn't like me getting in the way.'

'Yeah? I thought you'd patched all that up. He's happy with me now.'

'You sure? Yeah maybe he is but we've been writing all these songs, and I thought'

'Johnny, please. Don't think about breaking it up. It's working so good as it is'

He lowered his head, paused, chuckled quietly

'Well, yeah. Okay. We've like got something here, I know it. Just needs the right push.'

'Some things never change. You're picking it up fast - that's the way in - mixing, like when I-' -'Yes you told me. The days when Gene Pitney played tambourine on the Stones' album-' - 'O I am sorry. I'm boring you.'

'Fuck me Stella, leave it out, you sound like my sister.'

'What's she like, then?'

'Was. I haven't seen her in years. But she used to get really jumpy.'

'Maybe you could have been kinder.'

'Maybe, I dunno. Fuck, what do you know about it anyway? You-' 'Johnson. Slow down.'

He walked away across the room, sighed, looked at the wall. Turned back towards her. 'You don't need to tell me that. I'm not like that cunt. Ozzie.'

She half-smiled again. 'Ozzie!'

'It's all that Soho stuff I think we could make something of-'

'Soho stuff?'

'Yeah, the jazz, the real cool stuff.'

'Oh, honey, it's old news! It was never that cool anyway - guys trying to outblow each other, no room for the girls, and it hardly lasted any time.'

'Really?'

'Yeah, between the trad boom, I was too young for all that shit - and the funk stuff.'

'Hey there must have been more - it's all on record. And film too. The style, suits-'

'*Suits*? Are you serious? You wanna do a Sixties revival? Another one?

Stella thrust herself into the old armchair, curled her legs up

'Yeah, but strictly black-and-white and cool.' - 'Cool. You sound silly now. You don't really mean cool, do you? Like that?'

'Well, okay, I mean I want to use that style, put you in there. Maybe with just a bass. And percussion.'

'Hell, it could empty a room fast. But really it sounds like a godawful cabaret thing.'

'Why not?'

'Cabaret? I mean, in real life that's supper clubs, working men's pie clubs. Not Berlin.'

'Berlin...'

'Yes, you see the film?'

'Oh, yes. So, maybe it could be dark like that.'

'Well, all right, forget I said cabaret. But it still sounds old hat.'

'With these songs, though? Put a classic, uh, bebop, sound with post - new-wave attitude.'

He remained in centre-room; she uncurled herself, crossed to him and pressed her face on his chest, looked up- 'So you're the history man. You could be a manager.'

'Yah. I *like* doing the stuff - hussling and that - doing business.' -Half-closed his eyes, waving an air cigar, 'Baby, you gat star quality...' Stella looked hard into his eyes.

'Where the fuck did you get *that* from? You sound like someone else.'

Back in the old home for almost a week. It was cold, stale; but after a couple of days it was tolerable. Henry had returned because his instinct, which he usually mistrusted, led him to feel it would be best.

He hadn't heard from Richard since getting the 'book'. It was hardly a conventional accounts book; certainly nothing that would make much sense to an accountant with no sense of irony. Notes, dates, names; in uncertain order, covered nearly the entire book. One particular name cropped up most often; under "from". He had tried phoning Simon to see if there was any action, after he tired of getting no reply from Richard.

A low, gruff voice answered: 'Simon? He ain't ere. Uh, I dunno noffing.' -'Nothing, eh? What about-'

'Look, gettin' a new phone, so I'll call you when it's fixed, okay?' -'Well...' click

It was pure chance, seeing Parkin again: a pub in King Street, where he had gone instead of walking all the way along to a newly opened gallery, remembering that he couldn't get it up for galleries any more. He was halfway through a pint of Young's when he saw the boy, seated at a table fixed under the window. Parkin recognised him, all right, but he didn't have his usual brio. As Henry came over to join him he said, 'Hullo.' and shivered a little. 'You're with the Company right?'

'The what? Oh, look, I was with those people. I didn't even know who they were.

'What people?'

Henry realised he had almost blown it - Jerry wouldn't have seen his face, the day of the shooting.

'You're talking about the suppliers?'

'Yeah. The suppliers. They wanted to talk to you. Sorry, I had to tell im -tell em where you were. They said it was okay.'

Jerry Parkin's eyes shifted from side to side, his head lowered. He was suffering from withdrawal paranoia. Whenever Henry had seen him before, he had been cruising on enough speed to keep him happy. He shifted, getting ready to leave the window seat across the table from Henry; but Henry got up and sat beside him, blocking his escape. 'You can do me a little favour. I'll make it worth your while'

'Yeah, dunno about that. Can't do you any deals this week.'

'No, not that.' Henry reached into his inside breast pocket, producing a little paper wrap, which he laid beside Jerry's glass. 'Here, have this. On the house. It's *toot*, you call it.'

'Wao, man.' -Jerry slapped his hand down on the wrap and began standing up, but Henry applied a firm hold to his arm, pushing back down.

'Just tell me. Who is Collins?'

'C-Collins? You mean you don't know his name?'

'He's a connection. It's important.' - 'Connection? I thought he was running it.'

'Do you know where he is? His address?'

Jerry stared down wide-eyed at the table, his mouth slightly open. 'Don't you know?, Henry continued, 'Or are you just-'

'That shit about the dope coming from the coppers - it's shit. Everyone knows it's shit. Nuffing else.'

'Who said anything about them?
'Who?'
'The coppers.' -'I didn't. Just people been talking...' -'So we forget about the coppers. But you knew about Collins supplying it?'
'Don't know anyfing about im. Never saw im, eiver.'
'I just want to get sorted with him. I'm not going to say I saw you. Look at me. I just want the quiet life, like you, if you-'
'I can tell you someone who knows.' Jerry interrupted

CLIFF G HANLEY

Seven

It was an address Henry had visited two or three times with Simon. Really the suburbs, hidden in the vast maze of little terraces strung between Harrow Road and Queen's Park. He knocked on the door. No reply. It was an old door; perhaps the original, although it had been 'modernised' by the addition of a hardboard panel with two holes crudely added: one for letters, one to allow the old door handle to poke through. It was soggily soft to touch despite the layers of blue paint. He tried slapping it, hard, three times.

He stood back, looked at the bay window. No signs of anything beyond the matt finish of dirt, and a sheet tacked up in place of curtains. He looked round, as the bent-over figure of a skinny youth in oversize jeans, medium-length greasy hair, slouched past. 'Wastin your time there mite - they's gone away.' he muttered

'Oh.' answered Henry, who walked round to the archway passage leading through to the back. He remembered there had been a car parked in there before. Round at the back door he was just in time to catch a sight of the girl who lived here. But she saw him, too, and jumped back inside, slamming the door as she went. He waited patiently on the broken bits of tarmac, avoiding the grass, mud and dogshit.

'Angie! Look, I've not come for money! I'm just looking for a friend. Look, I've got some smokes.'

He could just make out her voice coming from indoors: *don't want smokes*

'Or snort. Look, I've got some wiz here. I'll leave it on the sill. Maybe see you in the pub.'

She made no sound. He left the little plastic bag on the kitchen window-sill, and quietly walked away. There was a pub just round the corner at the end of the street, where he settled down with a casual half of Guinness.

Later, when he returned, the bag had gone. 'Angie!' he shouted, once - looking up at the bedroom window. He waited for five minutes and decided to leave.

There had been no sign of activity in Borough; it seemed obvious that his 'little earner' was at an end, but he needed to find something to fill that gap in his life. And all the things he hadn't understood, all the things he hadn't been told, kept coming back to him in the small hours. And he still carried a deep resentment that he had allowed himself to be pressured into this in the first place. It added up to a desire to somehow rebalance the results. He resigned himself to living again in his Ladbroke Grove residence. One night he went out for a long walk. Summer was approaching; it was tolerably warm. He stopped for a pint at Bruce's, then continued northwards to Harrow Road, getting deliberately lost in the back streets and finally emerging in West Hampstead, to the broad north end of West End Lane.

'Hello dear, fancy some business?'

It took him a few seconds to take it in. The scrawny, skinny, dirty anxious little blonde; her thin voice. Business? Oh, yes. Oh, it's Angie! Lean forward, look closer. Even painted up, she looked older. She backed off

'Angie. Please. It's alright. I was just walking. Don't run off. Please.'

She had almost run, but instead of grabbing her arm he moved beside her. She stopped, but kept darting panicked looks around her. He pulled out his wallet.

'Here's a tenner. Take it easy, for god's sake. Can we sit down somewhere?'

'What the fuck do you want?'

'I want to find out who was running this show. The man I was working for, he wasn't really in charge.'

'Mr Collins?'

'No Rich- yes Mr Collins. I've... lost touch with him, that's all.'

'You're fucking pimping for 'im and you want *me* to help you? That's rich!'

'Pimping? Is that it?'

'Is that wot?'

'As far as I'm aware I've been dealing with rent arrears and - things like that. Look. Do I *look* like a pimp?'

She looked closer, her darkly sunken eyes taking him in. She almost smiled, but the smile faded fast as she half turned to run off again. 'Please! Don't tell him I grassed! I wasn't s'posed to know!'

'All right, all right. It's all right. So he's dealing in girls.' -'Yes! Fuckin illegals too. I gotta go. Can't stay 'ere.' -'Oh, Jesus. Here. Here's another twenty. Just tell me where I can find him. And here's a tissue for your eyes.'

Walking back home, ignoring the late traffic. Looking up at the terraces, uplit by the streetlights. Their eyes blind in shadow. He began leaving behind his impassive insensibility with each step; with each passing roar, each squeal of brakes in the confined passage of West End Lane. By the time he crossed into the tree-lined Chippenham Road he had walked off his regrets at caring too little, not just for - (too late) - Angela but for the other women who had brushed against his life. The edge of that warm sublimity touched his mind; the traffic once again retreated to the dim, · distant wall of noise, down by the horizon.

The number she gave him was for her minder.
'Hello, can I speak to Malcolm?'
'Eh, yeah.'
'Is that you Malcolm?'
'Wot - aw fack off' *'Wait* - That's Malcolm. Isn't it? Malcolm Birch?'
Malcolm was one of Henry's ex-students. The name he remembered; and now also the telephone voice.
'Malcolm. Listen. It's *Henry,* your old lecturer?'
'Wha - Henry? Not Enry Elly? You're pullin my fuckin leg.'
'I said, I just met a friend of yours.'
'Who?'
'Angie.'
'Jesus fuckin Christ. What're you doin with her then?'

'I met her. Never mind how. And I know you...
have an *arrangement* with her.'

'She told you, the fuckin... I look after her,
innit. She just pisses it away' 'Stop stop wait-
She told me nothing. I'm with the Company' -
'The fuckin company' -'Yes. And I have
contacts. I could maybe do you a favour. I just
want some information.'

Slam!

'H-Hello?'

He was angry enough to feel determined. The
pub where his students used to go when they
should have been listening to him. He spent a
week, sitting there every afternoon with a
paper, taking his time over a pint. Resulting in a
greatly improved knowledge about world
affairs, which he had always ignored
completely beyond the headlines; but no sign of
the boy. On the Friday, as he left, he recognised
Malcolm coming out of the bookie's and
crossing the road to another pub. He followed.
It was noisy, full of workers filling up with
'quick ones', and Malcolm was already deeply
in conversation with two others. Henry nearly
lost his nerve, but remembered how much
effort he had put into this already and strode
over, tapped Malcolm's shoulder.

'Wha? You?' -he was smiling at first but the
look became one of anger as he recognised
Henry. He threw himself forward and grabbed
Henry's arm as his chums looked on, bemused.
Henry found himself being manoeuvred into
the doorway before he was able to speak.

'Look, I know what you want. Take this-' he turned round to grab a beermat from the table inside the door, and, pulling a pencil-stub from his scratchy leather jacket, scribbled aggressively on it; thrust it at Henry. 'Well, thanks, how did-' 'Just take it and fuck off, yeah?'

'Ah, Trev, here you are!' - the gravel-voiced and florid Rob Norwich calling out as Trevor led The Slakers down into a basement-in-a-wall behind King's Cross Station; their new rehearsal room and also the headquarters of Blastoff T-shirts. 'Did you finish those royal punks?'

'Yes, they're here, in my case.' -'Good lad.'

'I didn't know you was an artist.' - Sam colliding into Trevor's back as the others descended, with Wiz at the end.

'Boys, this looks like some place you won't have trouble with neighbours.'

They were surrounded by racks of drying printed T-shirts: 'Adolf Hitler World Tour - cancellations', with just enough space in the middle of the floor, between printing beds, for the band to set up. Their organist had been folding and packing shirts for weeks before he coyly admitted an ability to draw cartoons. As Sam got his snare set up, sat down and gave it a trial bang, Rob gave a Stage Wince. 'Oh gawd, no, not that modern rubbish! Trev, look - here's the keys. I'm going to look round later to make sure you locked up.'

'Aw...' -'Really. You're a good kid, but this is a dodgy area. No point in taking chances. I'd stick around but I value my hearing! See you in the morning, Trev. Bye, everyone.'

The band collectively wishing their new landlord farewell, except for Johnson, who followed him up to the street.

'Ah, hey, Rob.' - catching up just as he was turning away to stride to his car, parked a street away- 'Listen. I've been thinking.'

Rob Norwich turned back towards Johnson, in guarded interest. 'Oho! The brains in the band. What have you been thinking about, then?'

'Well, we've got gigs lined up, quite a few. We do them as the band, and we got even more as backing band for a singer. She used to do jazz gigs but she writes her own stuff now. We play to a wide audience. We could promote those T-shirts.'

'So you kids are busy. That's excellent. Now why would you want to promote my shirts?'

'Would you consider a reduced rate for...'
'Reduced rate! I guessed you were going to get to that eventually.'
'Well, what do you say?'
Rob smiled broadly, tilted his head from side to side. 'Look, the rate I'm charging you barely covers the electricity.'
'What if we stored our gear here as well - we'd be paying you maybe a bit more.'
'A bit more. Yes. I'd have to give that some thought. As for now - if you kids are liable to be here when I'm not working, it will suit me to keep the place inhabited. I tell you what. Blastoff can be your official sponsors. If you can think of a way to shift the Ts at gigs that'll be a start.'
Johnson brightened; he almost began rubbing his hands. 'Oh, *good*. Like, Trev could design a band T-shirt too.'
'Okay! I'll print them for you. At a discount.'
'A disc...'
They looked at each other, smiling. Having established a certain amount of mutual respect. Johnson returned to the door as Rob Norwich raised his open palm in friendly acknowledgement.

The phone number extracted from Malcolm Birch turned out to be for an answering service. After three weeks of trying it, Henry gave up waiting for an answer and decided to try deciphering the scribbled numbers in The Book. He was convinced, perhaps out of desperation, that he had the right number.

'Hello?... May I speak to Mr Collins, please?'

'He don't live here any more.' - a mature West Indian lady replied and cut him off. Wrong number? Try again.

'...Hello? May I speak to Mr Collins please?'

'Look, this is being recorded, right, everything you say, and I'm going to report you, and you're going to be in *big trouble.*'

'Oh, I'm so sorry, I must have been given the wrong num...' *slam*

He tried another 'dead cert'.

'Mr Collins? May I ask your business?'

'Oh, I'm calling about the credit control thing, I was doing it, based in Borough, and I'd like to keep it going.'

'Credit *control*? What's your name?'

'Early. Henry Early. I was working for Richard.'

'Richard who?'

'With the big beard. The big suit.'

'The big suit...'(the stern, guarded voice taking on the colour of dry humour)-'O-okaay. Give me your number and I'll call you back.'

'About Mr Collins?'

'I'll call.'

It was the very last thing he expected, but the call would come two weeks later. In the meantime Henry, driven by curiosity and sheer boredom; and just a little forlorn hope of seeing that girl again, travelled back to Borough one darkly wet afternoon. Although Richard's floor was usually quiet, it felt more like the stillness of a corpse compared to that of a sleeper. He held his breath, walked up to his little flat. Opened the door. All was as he had left it, only three weeks before, although it seemed like more. The bag was where he had left it. He reached round the back of the kitchen tallboy to the hole-in-the-wall. Bag still there. He yanked it: his arm flew up as it came out with unexpected lightness. Empty. Stuck it in his saggy shoulderbrief and, putting on what he hoped was an impassive face, strode to the Tube station.

A gig for the Slakers alone: a basement club off Charing Cross Road. They had shared the night with an all-girl band, and the audience numbered fifty, mostly fans of the other band. The girls had packed up fast and got out; the boys were talking as they cleared the stage.

Sam was stowing his drums as quickly as he could, 'I'm fucked if I'm doing another one of these.'

'Yeh, fuckin pay-to-play,' added Trevor. 'No-one told you, you would get rich quick, boys-' put in Wiz as he lifted a cab off-stage, hugging it hard against his chest

'I'll admit I could do with a new bass-' Well it was a shit gig...' 'Thanks a fuckin bunch, it took me weeks phoning and sticking up fliers to get this-' 'Hahah, there you go, Nige, be grateful!' 'I gotta tell you now, I'm looking at doing a gig with Lucie.'

They stopped what they were doing, looked at Nigel. 'A gig? Just the one, then?' asked Johnson

'Yeah, well, maybe. We could like, do our own thing.' 'Wot, is it the-' 'No Sam it's the music.' - Johnson looked sceptical - 'I think really. I'm like getting into the electronic stuff.' Sam guffawed- 'Lucie's got a friend - she's blonde too - she can't really sing, but , I dunno, we could do a line-up...'

On the bus to Victoria, Henry thought a little more about what the kid, Parkin, had told him. And about what he had extracted from his ex-student. In the pub, not far from Victoria Bus Station, he soon found the quiet back room described on the phone.

A blond-haired man, obviously Collins by the look on his face, sat by the back wall, his eyes grimly fastened on Henry, who approached and sat, as Collins gestured wordlessly to the seat.

'Right. First things first. I got your message. If I understand what you said, it no longer counts. This comes down to a matter of trust. When people try to set up in business for themselves they are asking for trouble when they stray into others' territory.'

'You mean Richard.'

'Sears? He's out of the game now. And my advice to you is to remember what can happen if you don't behave.'

'I understand that he was cutting down on the drug business.'

'Business. I wouldn't know about that. He was a messenger boy, and he had no remit to go making decisions.'

Henry recognised Collins as the brown-haired man in the dark blue overcoat. 'Okay. Well, I think I passed you at his place'- aware of a heavily-built gent sitting down beside him- 'but I can keep it to myself.'

'I don't believe I've seen you before, anywhere. You trying to make some kind of point?'

'I'm aware that the real money is in the skin trade.'

'Skin trade? What's that?'

'Girls.'

'Oh... *Skin Trade.*' - He smiled sardonically- 'Whatever made you think that?'

'Whatever it is, I could have made something of it.' The heavy shuffled beside Henry, who looked round and noticed that he was almost the blond's twin except for his reddish hair- 'and coughed gently - 'I mean, I'm pretty discreet.'

Smiling coldly, 'Oh I bet you'll be discreet.' -He leaned forward. 'What business would that be?'

'What business? Your business, of course.'

'Our business - my business is my own business. You're a little out of your depth, and I would say that you're speaking out of turn.'

'Hey - I've seen what's going on. I've been round.'

'Round?' He smiled lazily at his cohort -'You can take it that you are not. In the company any more. Rien ne va pluss. Go back to your little cottage in King's Cross.'

'Well. Okay, I get the message, Mr Collins.'

The other sat back, 'Collins? You got it wrong, big time. No Mr Collins here.'

'But I spoke to him! He said-'

'He'll be... outside.' -He looked round, patted his chest. 'Look. We gotta go. I can give you a lift.'

'That's all right, really. It's a pleasant enough night.'

'You're giving us that book...yeah. '

'I might.'

'Well... pushy, aint we.'

'Well... I have it at home.'

The stranger remained impassive. His eyebrows had been punched hard enough to leave them permanently stupefied. Standing, he revealed himself as being only slightly taller than Henry. Outside the dimly lit pub, Henry turned in the direction of Victoria Tube. Quiet and dark; not quite late enough for the clubbers to have taken over the streets. The redhead blocked his way; the blond stood in his path for a moment before looking round towards someone, twenty feet away, a taller man in a dark coat - Collins? - who gave a slight gesture, and turned away. The heavies let Henry go and walked away towards Endell Street.

Back in Ladbroke Grove, he put off going home for an hour; sat in the Star for one half of lager followed by a pint of IPA. He walked slowly back up the road. The front door: fuck, the light was on, draining the bill.

His fingers tingled. He opened the door. Walked into the kitchen: as his eyes tuned themselves to the interior he became aware that all the books on his shelves had been pulled out and were heaped in mangled piles on the floor, facing up, facing down, pages ripped. Further: in the kitchen backroom most of his terracotta figures had been knocked over and smashed. He rubbed his forehead, 'Oh no, oh no, oh god, oh for fuck's sake'

His heart was pounding. He double-locked the front door, feverishly, knowing he was being mad. He found the remains of a half-bottle of gin, and filled a tall glass with tonic, topping it with the gin. The drink hardly helped him sleep. He decided to move out - at last - and remembered an estate agent being up in Great Western Road. He could do it first thing in the morning.

While grey morning faded out of night, work began on setting up Trevor's 'installation'. Under the concrete flyovers of the Westway at Little Venice, a box, six feet high, four wide and ten long - covered in darkred fake fur. A crowd of sixty, all in black coats except for a few quilted anoraks, plus Nigel and his blonde, in matching baggy jeans and purple sweaters. She had giant false eyelashes; he wore discreet mascara. Stella and Johnson. And two safety officers. Two girls in wide-brimmed black hats. So much black: a little like a church outing except for the media people. A handful of men with giant lenses flash indiscriminately, at the box and at the crowd. A small table is set up with plastic cups and bottles of cheap /champagne', being dispensed by an unhappy youth in a baggy grey hooded top. Trevor, in his usual black padded spaceman jacket, jeans and trainers, circles the Box with two friends in regulation anoraks, baseball caps and oversized jeans, looking up at it, and occasionally at some of the babbling guests, who are not interested in unknown kids as much as networking or getting close to the man in secret-police glasses, rumoured to be from the Tate, for a photo-opportunity. Rob Norwich, his back to the murmuring throng, gives an interview to the mobile TV camera team, as sponsor of the event. 'Certainly. Trevor's an exceptionally talented young lad, coming from practically nowhere, and I feel quite privileged to have been able to pull the strings necessary to make this possible. We at Blastoff look forward to yet doing more promotion of the arts in the near future. And-' (looking round as a muffled boom interrupts) 'here we go!'

The fake fur erupts in a ball of flame. To a great shout and squeals from the multitude. In five minutes it blackens and peels off to a perspex inner tank filled with water. The plastic melts. There is screaming. The water bulges out of the base, soaking the lower legs of those who are unable to jump backwards fast enough. Screams. Revealed: a twice scaled-up see-through plastic chair.

Saturday was bright, almost sunny. Henry looked up at the scrubby sky from the kitchen. He had spent a bad night on the couch. He could hardly face even a cup of tea yet; it was ten already - he should aim for the Agent's shop. But as he thought this there was a grinding, squeaking noise from the front door; a bang as it flew open. Boots clattering on his floorboards. He pressed back against the wall behind the kitchen table as Collins and his men filled the room, Collins coming in last, having shut the door. He held a small gun at his side.

'Right.' he said.

'Right, what?', Henry stepped forward

The red-haired heavy punched Henry so hard in his chest, with the flat of both hands, that he sprawled on the floor among the remains of his sculptures.

'We could just take you out.' he growled

'And you only have Richard's word that the fucking book is here!' Henry gasped

Collins spoke up, quietly: 'You didn't deny it. I'm a reasonable man-' Henry began laughing 'and I can assure you that I have your interest at heart. This is about mutual advantage.'

Henry stopped laughing abruptly as Collins' voice took on a threatening tone, 'You can trust me.'

'It's in here,' Henry said as he got to his feet, steadied himself on the table's corner and hobbled towards the backroom. The three others followed and he stood on a chair, reaching up to the wall. As Collins passed under the shadowy ceiling Henry yanked on a rope, the ornamental rock flew down and smashed into Collin's head, grazing one side as he jumped backwards. His gun went off, the bullet entering the red-head's leg. With a yell of pain he fell against the wall. The other ran forward towards Henry, who had sidled round to the sink and grabbed his favourite Stanley knife. He had enough anger bottled up to keep him going: he stepped forward to meet the man with a thrust, catching the blond's up-raised fist and slashing deep into his forearm. As Collins dragged himself out through the door to the hallway, both the men hit down on Henry; He found himself being thrown out of the first-floor window to land on the softly rotting wooden lean-to shed. He rolled over and half-fell, half-dropped to the ground. It was raining heavily, and he was already soaked. Inside the house, the red-head was sobbing in pain; he reached down to pick up the gun, and fell against the blond.

'Fuck! I can't fuckin see with this in my leg!'

'Gerroff! You're bleeding!'cried the blond

'Gotta lie down! Fuck! Outa here!'

'Yeah well fuck Collins!'

'And the fuckin artist!'

Henry half-fell, half-dropped from the roof. At the side of the house, there was hardly more than a car's width between it and the next wall. He turned away to the road and his car, yanked the 2CV door open and threw himself in. As he turned back towards the side of the house he put the headlights on full. He could see Collins now from behind the wheel although the rain was hammering off the bonnet; he was sneaking across the back wall by the bins down the side. Henry got in gear, jammed his foot down...

'Hey, Stella. It's Oscar.'
Johnson, sprawled on the new mattress, chopping a line on a small circular mirror while watching the small TV settled on the straw matting covering most of the floor
'Oh, fuck it, I was sleeping.' - Stella running her fingers through her hair as she entered
'It's the dope - you could do less.'
'Smoking that stuff - you sound like Ronnie Scott'
'Ro-'
'Anyway it's better for you than that creepy speed.'
'Ain't wiz - it's C.'
Stella joining him on the floor of their Kilburn Housing Association flat. Looking.
'It's nothing - some kinda history thing.' - he continued chopping

'It's a resumé of their first year, that's what it is.' -pushing her hair out of her face, she reached out, turning up the volume

'...although at the same time, sceptics have suggested that Tony Blair should be leading the *Labor* Party. Well, that's the round-up of our first colourful and exciting six months, serving London.'

*

For mash get Smash

*

Raffles - one step ahead

*

Get away people

*

For every bottle they export, a Bavarian sheds a tear

*

Advaunced heah caah

*

(swirling patterns, big music) The News!

Camera pans in on desk with Deborah Brooks

'The headlines today: Georgia: with access to the Black Sea ports cut off, Eduard Shevardnadze has capitulated, and the latest in the Borough Gangster Investigation.'

Cut to

Film of tenement / syringes / bunches of five-pound-notes / Richard escorted into police van / police officer holding up open palm to blank out camera

Voice over:

'The latest revelations in the Borough area of London reveal that this was an organisation that had connections, or at least interests, in many other parts of the city. Investigating officers have made it clear that although the man originally apprehended and now in a coma in St Thomas' Hospital has been identified as Richard Sears, he is not the *Mister Big*, and that there may be yet another pulling the strings. They are unable to comment about the allegations of police collusion.'

CLIFF G HANLEY

Flatulent for Fifteen Minutes

Ronald Parkview, whose family of humble roots in Workington prospered under the Rule of Quango in the early years of the Third Millenium, found that no amount of inherited wealth would render him impervious to cancer, although that ailment was on the very edge of being consigned to history. He was forced to undergo treatment which culminated in surgery; a transplant of the terminal section of his large intestine.

To his incalculable relief, the operation was a success, and after a considerable time recuperating in the best hospital that money could buy, he was able to return to his home in Kent, South London.

It had taken Ronald some time coming to terms with utilising his new and alien body part but he was glad to be able to witness its regular efficiency -in fact if anything the new aperture was perhaps a little more efficient than he would have preferred.

This minor inconvenience, however, was soon eclipsed by a baffling new phenomenon. On rising one morning and making his way into his bathroom, Ronald was puzzled to hear a muffled muttering - perhaps, he thought, from outside his bedroom door. He froze. The muttering stopped. He crossed the bedroom and threw open the door.
There was no one there.
He continued attending to his toilette. In the bathroom he could hear once again that strange incomprehensible muttering. It seemed now to be coming from below. He bent down to the floor. It got louder; but now its source was somewhere behind him.

For several weeks Roland was tormented by the mystery voice. Eventually he was forced to admit that not only was it not an intruder: it was not, as he had subsequently hoped, an auditory hallucination caused by some shift in perception, or (not that he would hope for such in normal circumstances, but any explanation built on accepted norms of pathology and logic would have been a relief) a neurological short-circuit. The sound was emanating from Ronald's own rectum.

His doctor, when summoned and informed of the problem, was so sceptical as to be angry despite Ronald's haggard and unshaven appearance, but as soon as the victim walked across the bedroom to which his world had shrunk, visited only by his manservant, the good doctor apologised profusely and immediately set about calling the surgeon who had performed Ronald's operation. He avoided giving out too many details on his RistfoneTM , but was able to communicate a sense of urgency to Mr Canning, who would normally have been unavailable for six months, but who appeared early that very evening. Of course the surgeon went through the same litany of reactions: bemusement, anger, embarrassment and astonishment.

'D'you know, Chingford, knowing you from the club, I wouldn't have put this past you. But now...'

"Now?' asked Chingford

'Now - I feel it has the ring of truth about it.'

'Well, Canning, do you think you would be able to throw some light on this?' asked Dr Chingford, sitting back in Ronald's easy chair as Canning stood in the window, rubbing his scalp.

'Perhaps, perhaps. Let's see. It's irregular to do this, of course, but - well "- Canning gave Chingford a single conspiratorial wide-eye - "we could summon up the facts right here.'

He sat down on the edge of Ronald's bed and brought out his tablet.

"Ah...yes...here we are. The donor. Male. Um... Yes. Look at that. Nothing pathological; died of old age."

'But...Does that mean there is no explanation?' trembled Ronald.

"Who was the donor anyway?" asked Dr Chingford.

'Ah yes that's possible.' replied Mr Canning, 'Right. Here we have it.'

His fingers tapped and squeaked on the tablet.

'Here. He was an artist, of some sort.'

'Anyone, famous?' asked Ronald.

'Well...his name...Cliff G... Hanley. Famous? I couldn't say.' He looked up, half-smiled and shrugged apologetically, ' I really couldn't say. I haven't heard of him, anyway.'

CLIFF G HANLEY

Being Jeremy

Jeremy was really ill. He couldn't tell if it was the drink, or that bloody seafood.

'Jeremy! What's up with you? You've been snoring all night, and it's late,' Samantha whined, her voice a gravelly intrusion on Jeremy's determination to avoid beginning the day. Another bloody day. 'Oh no, leave it out Sam. I'm really sick. That horrible fish food-' 'You mean the oysters?' 'Oh please, even the word! Don't say it. Must have been that. I don't snore. Do I?'

'Don't be silly. If they'd made you ill it would have been last night. Yes, you do, you know.'

He rolled off the bed to the floor, leant against the bathroom door for a while. Samantha, fully dressed, began bustling round the little kitchen. The dog, a little terrier, roused himself from his basket, tail wagging, and enthusiastically ran round her as she reached down some food, wielding the tin opener and emptying the contents into his bowl. 'You bad boy! They'd think I was starving you. Naughty boy.' Stroking his head as he dug his face into the gourmet meat. Digdigdig...

Jeremy decided he wasn't, after all, going to throw up. He decided to experiment with a bowl of cornflakes. The box was there, on the kitchen table. He sat down. Elbows on the table. Ran his fingers through his hair. Easy enough to turn in the chair and extract the milk carton from the fridge. Poured it in. Mashed the cornflakes. Samantha had stopped petting the animal, and could see what he was doing. He knew she would say something. She always did.

'Eugh! I thought you'd stopped tha...

'Hurry up now, just time for a cuppa tea. And don't play with your food! Dad doesn't play with his food'

'Mum doesn't mind.' - he picked at the blistered paint on the side of his chair - it wasn't a blister, he knew - blisters were fun: either to burst or pick at; but it was nosepick - his own maybe...

'Mind? Of course she minds! And anyway it'll be time for the bus at half past.'

Jeremy's big sister was ten years old, almost twice his age, and she reminded him of this whenever possible.

She resented his being spoiled as the 'baby' of the family.

'You'll both be late, if you keep on arguing. Go on, Jerry, finish up,' their mother interrupted from the kitchen, 'and it would be better for me if you two went out when your father goes too.'He muttered, through a mouthful of mashed food, 'I can get the other bus anyway...'

'Bus? What on earth are you talking about? The car-' 'Bus? I said I could get. No. I was... somewhere else. I think.'

Samantha leaned her back against the fridge, folded her arms. 'You really are out of it today. Are you being serious?'

'Oh, well. Yes. Look, I could really use a coffee.'

' There's nearly a cup here in the jug.' - Samantha poured out the last of the coffee. Jeremy topped it with a little milk and gratefully drank it down.

'I don't know. It's a feeling, like being sick-' 'Sick!' 'no, really, like being sick. Nausea maybe a better word. It's confusing. I thought I was back at home, going to school.'

'Sleeping with your eyes open? S'not as if you don't sleep enough.'

'Wossa time?'

'God, it's time I was off. Don't worry about us, I can walk to the office. Mavis isn't in today anyway, so...'

'Thanks. Feel a bit ropey. Maybe a shower, I'll be okay to drive in later.'

'Why don't you take it easy? I mean, you had this before. Remember after the new contract. I thought it was because of that party.'

'I wasn't even at the party.'

Samantha gathered up Joey and turned towards the door. He got up and followed them; was about to peck her on the cheek when Joey, his head resting on her shoulder, gave him a sharp little woof. He let them go.

A week later, as he was driving to work after dropping his girlfriend and that bloody animal off at the 'Centre', he had to take a different route from the usual one: a police car and an ambulance were blocking the entrance to the street, first left. Apart from that, life went on as normal. Jeremy, Samantha and... it was baffling him that she had fancied getting a dog in the first place. In the shop, they were all pretty much the same to him. But he could happily admit that he hated the little animal. Didn't feel much love for her either, these days. His 'girlfriend'. Somehow their little flat wasn't really home as it should be.

The following day, he scanned the paper for news about the accident in the street. It was a nuisance, having to change routine. There was nothing in the paper. Jeremy had mentioned it at the office. 'An accident? Charlie, the accountant, said, 'not round here, surely?'

'Well, yes, it must have been one. Cop cars, ambulances, the lot.'

'This morning? Dunno how I could have missed that one!'

After giving Samantha a deeply searching kiss, ignoring the yipping and whining of the dog, Jeremy let them out at the Centre and drove on. Second right, first left: he felt a premonition of terror; everything went white. He seemed to be getting drawn backwards and it was terrifying. It stopped.

Joey looked up. He didn't really feel like going for a walk. Splashing in puddles was fine, but he never liked the rain. It annoyed his back. Rolled his eyes at Samantha. It always worked.

'Oh dear you poor little soul! Come to mummy.'

She bent down to him, picked him up and enfolded him between her plump arms and ample breasts. He opened his mouth wide, waggling his tongue and half-closing his eyes. His lead hung down from his collar, waving around below, unnoticed. The man was watching them. He didn't care. He liked being a dog, being spoiled, being babied.

He liked his new name too. Joey. Better than the old one.

CLIFF G HANLEY

The Last Supper

First published in Decode Magazine

REPLAY> It started, really, in the interstice between the morning chill and the first yawning of the sun, as the honeysuckle gas clouds filled my garden; the palpable fragrance drifting in through my window.

The whole day seemed nostalgically back-lit. It is difficult to be sure about this, as we tend to remember our memories, which in turn call up their memories: memory fleas piggy-backing ad infinitum.

But later, As we climbed up and out of the traffic-choked city, it began to rain; a warm light rain, hardly more than mist, really, but enough to tamp down the city dust and cool our skins. It passed, leaving the smell of warm summer dust.

As we sprawled carelessly on the wet grass up on the Downs, the red sunset over Wales endlessly fed our endlessly lustful appetites. Our salad of anchovies, seeds, olives and peppers with sun-dried tomato bread had not deadened our senses with that satiated feeling that might come after, say, a winter vindaloo; by a miracle of packaging technology we were able to enjoy hand-made Italian ice cream next. The chianti sparkled in our throats and in our minds and cleared our palettes in readiness for the strawberries.

The strawberries, red in our mouths and never-ending, as the picnic cloth became a bed sheet. Your tongue became another fruit as we joined together, sighing ecstatically under a red sky. Far up and away in the top edge of that sky flew a tiny silver plane, catching a flicker of sun. The lights went off.

REPLAY> It started